VENOMOUS

THE HUNT FOR VENGEANCE

RICHARD J PERSONS II

Auctorem House
276 5th Ave, Ste 704-2591
New York, NY 10001
www.auctoremhouse.com
1.888.332.7718

**Dedicated with love to my mother
Maria De La Luz Gonzalez Gonzalez Persons**

With Special Thanks to:

Thomas J. Herrera
Frank Gonzales
and
Sifu Dave Meadows
For their encouragement, and support.

To my Father in heaven, where my eyes have become one in
perfect unity, filled with the light of Your love.
With all my heart, in Jesus Christ.

CHAPTER

ONE

**PRESENT DAY
NEW YORK CITY**

STEPHANIE HURRIED OUT of the grocery store, groceries in one hand and her son Jeremy, clutched in her other arm. Stephanie is a young 22-year-old single mom with the qualms of everyday living on her mind. As she reached her car she sat Jeremy down with a warning to stay close.

"Where are those keys? Jeremy, did you take mama's keys? Oh, here they are." She scooped up her groceries and put them in the back of the station wagon. She was just tightening the last strap on Jeremy's car seat when she heard voices behind her. "Gimme the keys and back off, lady. Then nobody gets hurt."

Stephanie bolted up quickly, knocking her head on the door of the car. She spun around to see two large and scruffy looking men staring at her. One had a small gun pointed at her and the other had his hand at the edge of his pocket, as if he were hiding something.

"Didn't you hear me bitch? I said give me the damn keys—NOW!!"

Stephanie handed over the keys and stood motionless. Her mind was a total blank. She backed slowly away from the car and then stopped every fiber of her being focused on her child. Jeremy wailed from his seat. "Mama no go! Mama no goooooo!

"Shit... she's got a kid in there."

One of the men pulled Jeremy roughly from the car and pushed him toward his mother. He toddled to her as fast as his two-year-old legs would carry him. "Please... please don't take my car! I don't have any insurance... I, I don't have a lot of money.... You won't get anything for it... please!!"

Her panic rose to an uncontrollable level and she began to cry hysterically.

Joe Jeager was about to turn on the ignition when he heard the screams. Immediately on his guard, he looked around and noticed a woman on her knees, clutching a toddler about two cars down from him. He could see one man with a gun but was unsure if there were any others on the scene. Slowly he climbed out of his sports car. After quickly pulling off several rings and sliding them into his shirt pocket, he adjusted his maroon and black pin-stripe tie. Pulling at the lapels of his Italian made sports coat, he glanced at his silk maroon shirt and smiled knowing he looked much better than the day before. Joe was always a sharp dresser. With his inherently good looks, he found that dressing like that gave him an air of authority over the people around him. He knew that his light brown, clean-cut hair made his piercing blue eyes and squared features stand out. With his mind focused on the job at hand, and keeping his body low to the ground, he circled and came up behind the man holding the gun and Stephanie's keys who was just about to start the car.

Joe stood up and tapped the would-be car-jacker coolly on the shoulder. "Excuse me, sir. Why do you have the lady's keys?" The car-jacker spun around and aimed the gun directly at Joe's face. Nonplused,

Joe pushed the gun to his left with his right hand and keeping it there, at the same time bringing his left hand underneath the barrel, causing the gun to point back into the stranger's face. "Shit, man, what're you tryin' to do? kill me?" "Better you than me," Joe replied.

The car-jacker let go of the gun and tried to throw his hands up in the air as Joe sharply belted him in the jaw, knocking him senseless.

Joe pulled the thief out of the car, stepped over his unconscious body and walked toward the rear of the automobile where the other man now had Stephanie by the hair, a knife wedged against her throat. "Move, bitch, or I'll gut you and the little rug rat right here, you got me?"

With his other hand he rummaged through her purse that was resting on a nearby car. Jeremy was sitting near the rear tire, crying.

Joe walked slowly toward the mugger, who was obviously very nervous by this time. "Take the purse if you need it that bad, man. Just leave the lady and her boy alone."

The thief kept a close eye on Joe as he continued to rummage through the bag. "You keep coming closer and this whore dies. Back off, asshole!"

"Come on, let her go. Then no one will get hurt."

The mugger tightened his hold on Stephanie. The knife scratched at her tender skin, leaving a tiny trickle of blood.

"So you want to be a hero asshole. Let's see what you got"

The mugger, sucking on a wad of snuff, spit at Joe's feet, sizing up his opponent, unable to determine if this sharp dressed man posed any threat.

"You may have beaten that dumb son of a bitch, but I'm getting what I came for. And maybe a little bonus. You ain't shit!"

His free hand reached around Stephanie and squeezed her breast suggestively as he licked the side of her face. She screamed and the mugger leered. "I just as soon kill her as screw her. Makes no difference to me."

"Don't do it. Look, I'm putting the gun down. Just let her go." Joe set the gun down slowly and then slid it under the front of the car next to him with his foot before the thug could tell him to slide the weapon toward himself.

The mugger threw Stephanie to the ground and she lay there stunned. She looked up slowly and saw the mugger smile at the man who had thrown down the gun. She pulled herself toward Jeremy and the car. Her knees were raw and she could feel the blood dribbling down her neck. But she was alive.

Joe faced the assailant, his arms extended palms upward. He began to back away slowly, giving an air of submission to his movements. The mugger lunged at Joe, attempting to stab him with the knife. Joe struck the aggressor at a pressure point just below the ear knocking the blade from the attacker's hand. The assailant's body convulsed and he defecated on himself as his limp body hit the pavement. Joe walked over to Stephanie and helped her up from the pavement. "Are you all right, miss?"

"Yes, yes, I think so. Thank you... God... thank you so much!"

She threw her arms around Joe's neck and he blushed, embarrassed by her display. He felt a tug on his pant leg and looked down to see Jeremy pointing at the fallen mugger.

"Mama, Mama!" he replied. "Bad man make a poo-poo!"

Joe and Stephanie laughed as a crowd gathered around the scene.

TWO

PRESENT DAY SOMEWHERE IN ALASKA

PUSHING THROUGH THE shipping lanes was a gargantuan cargo freighter, the Neptuni Regis, known for its ice breaking abilities. On this day, the sun was shining bright. A cool breeze came from the southeast making it very pleasurable to be outside. Above, the sky was a perfect, deceptively blue, and a cool breeze carried the sharp scent of salt and metal across the deck. On the fantail of the ship lounged a group of sailors. John O'Sullivan was fast asleep on a chair propped up on two legs against a newly painted bulkhead. Several of his shipmates were sick and tired of him constantly shirking, about not getting his work completed. They were upset because the entire department would get punished for his laziness. They had continually threatened that if he did not do his part, he would pay for it in other ways. Sensing the opportunity for retribution they gently placed a palm full of used, smelly, bearing grease, that stunk worse than the ship's clogged bilge in one of O'Sullivan's outstretched, slacken hands.

Stacy Keystone, the on-board comedian, shushed giggling comrades as he took a shoelace off of O'Sullivan's boot. With a mischievous grin, he took the crusty shoelace and placed it over O'Sullivan's face, trying his best not to laugh at the sight of his victim's face. John O'Sullivan's eyes were slightly opened, just enough to see the whites. His mouth draped open with a puddle of spit forming at the edge of his lips waiting to flood over onto his chin. John O'Sullivan shrugged his shoulders slightly as Stacy brushed the edge of his cheek with the shoelace. With a quick slap, O'Sullivan swung his grease-covered hand to his face to brush off any "insects" that might be nesting on his face. Splat went the grease as Stacy stepped back, unable to avoid the splatter of goop to his dungarees. A heavy coat of the oil was smeared into John O'Sullivan's mouth, nostrils, and right eye. Tasting the grease, he roared out of his stupor, "What the hell! What the hell!!? What the hell are you doing to me!!!!?"

He screamed as the sensation of small, hot needles being pushed through his eye galvanized him into action. Jumping to his feet, he ran toward an entrance to the starboard-side aft corridor. Unable to see clearly, he crashed into a door braced by a bulkhead, bloodying his nose. He mewled his anger and frustration, running down the corridor to a nearby head to wash his eyes out. Laughing hysterically amongst each other, the crew members were high-fiving one another.

"We warned the son-of-a-bitch" one of them shouted.

"You think the dumb bastard will sleep on the job again?" another spouted.

Grueber leaned against a nearby railing smoking a Marijuana cigarette (joint). He wore an authentic WWII Nazi Officers P-Coat. Over the past several months at sea, the black suede coat had grown dingy and stained from oily dirt and spilled beer, the gold buttons faded from the salty sea air. His forehead bared a small, distinct swastika, an emblem he at one time wore proudly as a ranking member of the Aryan Brotherhood. Now it was a reminder of a time in his life he'd been trying to forget.

He passed the joint to his best friend, Pugh, a full-blooded, dark skinned Jamaican sporting dirty and matted dreadlocks.

Before inhaling the intoxicating smoke, Pugh turned to his neo-Nazi friend and laughed, "Hey mon, when ya gonna let me do dat beautiful blondie a yours? I'm tired a jacken off to that picture of her white, round ass on your bunk, mon."

"Shit. I'd rather fuck a blender than have you stick your diseased, black boner in her powdery white ass," snickered the former skinhead.

They both roared with laughter, the sound blending with the low hum of the ship's engines. They cranked up the forecast on the radio. The announcer was intoning. "Another record high in the temperature forecasted for today, somewhere in the lower 80s. Another earthquake reported last night, registering 4.5 on the Richter scale. Grey skies are approaching so beware."

Just then the ship passed near large walls of bluish-gray ice. Huge chunks slapped into the ocean as Pugh gets the attention of his good buddy. "Hey mon. Look at dat. Isn't dat a beautiful sight, mon?!" "Incredible man!!!" stated Grueber. Both are very intoxicated and in a stupor.

Again, over the radio the announcer warned, "Be on the lookout for icebergs. We don't want repeats of the Titanic."

Ironically, just after the announcement, the hull of the ship echoed as the ship smashed against some large object, filling the halls of the ship with a strange vibration. Which every sailor on board could feel it to the bone. Everyone on the deck of the ship rushed to see what caused the vibration. Pugh looked over the side of the ship just in time to see an iceberg splitting into several chunks. The largest of the masses rolled over, exposing a beautiful cylindrical object buried in the ice.

"Mon, did you see dat?" the wasted Jamaican asked.

"See what!" yelled Grueber.

"That, mon, open your eyes. Over there. Dat purple ting in da ice," spouted Pugh.

"Mon, I bet dat would buy a lifetime worth of ganja for da both of us."

Stoned out of his gourd, he yells, "Give me dat three-pound hammer of yours. I'm goin' for it, mon."

"Are you freaken crazy? The drop alone will kill you, ya stupid Jamaican dumb ass. I ain't losing my best friend over something stupid like that. That drop is over a hundred feet down. The ice-covered water would be like landing on concrete. Not to mention the Hyperthermia you stupid ass, you will die within minutes of hitting the water."

Oh, ya, mon, you're right. I don't know what da hell I was tinkin," sighed Pugh.

They both watched as the current carried the object slowly toward the open ocean and warmer waters.

LONG BEACH, NEW YORK

"I said gimme your money, you little shit!"

Jesse's ears rang as he was hurled against the lockers. "Geez, Tony! I told you I don't have any money today! Can't you guys just leave me alone?" Tony sneered, leaning in closer until Jesse could smell the stale stink of his breath. "No way, Jesse. You are just too easy." mocked the bully. His voice dripping with cruelty

The four boys behind Tony laughed as they nodded their heads in agreement. Tony rifled through Jesse's pockets and was rewarded with two crumpled up dollar bills and a half pack of chewed gum. Tony held them up mockingly, shaking his head in fake disappointment.

"That's it? You're pathetic."

As they walked away, one of the boys gave Jesse a final smack to the head.

Jesse straightened his clothes and picked up his books as another group of boys approached him. "Are you ready for your initiation after school?" asked a voice from behind.

Jesse rubbed his forehead and nodded to the boy, whom he knew as Miguel. His head was throbbing terribly. At this rate, he'd never make it to sixth grade English.

"Good. When you pass the initiation, you'll be one of us. Then those jerks won't bother you anymore."

Miguel and the others turned and walked away, staring in the direction of the five jerks walking away with Jesse's lunch money. Jesse leaned against his locker and sighed.

C H A P T E R

THREE

JOSHUA ROGERS WAS a blithe man. After 65 years of being a fisherman he had finally bagged the big one off the coast of Long Beach New York. One morning's work and he had a check in his hands for $250,000 and a half ton of tiger shark on his hook. A photographer yelled out at Joshua. "Hey there old man! Can you tell us how you bagged the big one?" Joshua responded "I figurrd da $20 entra fee was worth da chance at da $250,000 prize moneys. And for once in my life, I be right." Joshua was more than happy to oblige. He grinned a toothless grin at the crowd. His leathery old face told a few stories of its own. In the crowd another photographer burst out to Joshua. "Give us a smile for the morning paper and tell us what you're going to do with all that money." Joshua replied with a big toothless grin. "First thin I gunna do is get me some real teef." Down in the center of the crowd the neighborhood boys were grinning and punching at each other. Trying to contain themselves for nightfall.

Inside the meat locker Joshua accompanied the fishing judges as his prize shark was placed in a huge meat locker to await processing. Joshua patted the shark's belly as it hung in the meat locker, talking to the shark "Well, old friend, I reckon I'll see ya in the mornin." Night was falling as the men left the storage facility. They didn't notice the three boys lurking in the shadows outside.

"Are they gone, Jesse?" asked Trudy.

"Yeah, Trudy, I think they are."

Jesse was nervous. He knew that they could get into a lot of trouble for what they were about to do.

"Then have at it," whispered one of the delinquents.

Miguel handed Jesse a large carving knife. He stood there with his hands on his hips, issuing a silent challenge to Jesse.

Jesse walked very slowly to the door of the meat locker. Luckily, the men had hung the keys in plain sight. Once inside, Jesse stared at the huge shark draped on a large meat hook in this cold room. He was so scared that he didn't think he could move. Then one of the older boys pushed him toward the shark. Jesse held his breath and plunged the knife into the belly of the huge fish. He cut it open from jaw to tail, gagging at the smell. Bloody water poured out of the shark's stomach along with a few curious objects, including fishing line, an old bicycle tire, a fairly recent Playboy magazine, and a little girl's doll. One of the boys immediately grabbed the magazine while the others stayed back, complaining about the smell. Jesse dropped the knife and put both hands on the belly of the shark, spreading it wide open to make sure there was nothing left inside. As he did so, a round, bloody object fell to the floor and rolled toward the corner of the room. Jesse inched to where the object had rolled and he picked it up. He rubbed it on his shirt to get the blood off and then held it up for his friends to see. It was the size of a grapefruit and made from a hard crystal, it looks ancient and with-in the crystal was a Florissant purple and black color trying to mix but unable to. The crystal had four dragon heads with marking that appeared to be from the orient.

"Shit! What is that thing?" Miguel asked incredulously. "I bet its worth some money. Give it here."

He grabbed at the container, but Jesse pulled away from him, dropping it in the process. The top of the container cracked and an acrid smoke filled the air. Through the smoke, the boys could see a light begin to glisten. Jesse leaned closer to get a better look as the light shone bright on his face. The other boys were overcome by the smoke and stench in the room and began to vomit violently. The three boys tried to run from the room to get some fresh air but continued to be sick. The smell of rotting meat and eggs seemed to be everywhere. The doors flew open as one by one the boys spilled out. First was Miguel, then Trudy, and last was Jesse. As the boys caught their breath, Miguel and Trudy turned and looked at Jesse. "Oh my god!" Miguel cried. "Jesse, you look like crap!"

Trudy turned away from his friends. "I'm getting the hell out of here."

The boys all took off, running frantically away from the horrible stench. Jesse ran for home as fast as he could. The vomiting had stopped but he still felt that something was very wrong. Every once in a while, he caught a look at his reflection in a store window and cringed. His skin had turned a pasty white, his eyes sunken and bruised. His lips were swollen and chapped.

There were no lights on as he walked into his house. "Mom? Dad? Anyone home?" he muttered.

Jesse felt a sense of relief when no one answered his call. He didn't want to explain why he smelled or looked the way he did. He ran upstairs to the bathroom and took a quick shower. The stench seemed to cling to him though, no matter how hard he scrubbed. As he dried himself off the feeling of hunger struck him very hard. He hid his ruined clothing under his bed and then headed downstairs. In lustful haste, he feverishly rushed down to the basement refrigerator that housed the weekend feast for his dad's birthday. There, wrapped in plastic suspended in yellowish internal fluids, were two pig's heads, eyeballs blankly staring into space. His dad had developed a taste for this exotic feast while stationed in a secret base deep in the heart of Brazil.

Shaking with anticipation, he lunged towards the refrigerator handle only to be greeted by an unfamiliar sting. Propelled back by an unknown force, his hand crashed into a nearby wall. Still in an uncontrollable lust, he reached again for the handle. As before, his hand was propelled back. This time the force was so violent that it sent his limp appendage tearing through a nearby wall. His arm now dangling at his side, he momentarily paused to regain the sensation in his arm. He looked at his weakened arm, tingling with pain. To his amazement, blue strings of electricity were dancing from finger to finger. He began to giggle as the currents tickled the tips of his fingers. Realizing that he could not make contact with his bare hands, he wrapped them with a shop rag and attempted to open the refrigerator once again. He flung the door open, grinning at his clever success. There before him sat the items which drove his lustful hunger. After a moment's pause, his head jerked several times as his jaw was forced open. His human teeth folded back on themselves, making way for the beast's jagged fangs. With the hunger of a starving dog, he attacked the pig's head encased in polyurethane. A low chalky grind accompanied by an occasional pop echoed through the basement walls as Jesse ground his gaping maw into the plump flesh of the pig, striking the cheek bone. Several minutes into his feeding frenzy, he began to realize just how grotesque his actions were. He could not help but continue with his morbid feast until it was fully consumed, as disgusting as this now seemed to him. Realizing just how taboo his actions were, he slowly backed to the stairs.

Then, as if to escape from himself, he ascended the stairs.

Jesse washed his hands and face with hot water and soap in an attempt to conceal his blasphemous act. No matter how hard he tried traces of blood and bits of raw flesh smeared his face and hands. He looked even worse than before. His reflection in the mirror terrified him and he began to try to calm down by talking out loud to himself.

"Jesse, old boy, you're just having a really bad day. Just clean yourself up and go to bed. This may even be a dream. Write mom and dad a note and go to bed. They'll never know the difference. And when you wake up in the morning everything will be fine. Just fine. Normal. No more weird shit."

He wrote a fast note to his parents and climbed into bed.

"Jesse? Honey, are you home?" Jesse's mother Christine walked into the kitchen and saw the note on the counter:

"Mom and Dad
I've eaten already and done my
homework. I'm very tired.
Went to bed
Love, Jesse"

FOUR

"I GUESS HE was really worn out tonight, Steve. Those boys at school have been picking on him again. Poor kid. I'll check on him later. Are you hungry? I can make us something."

After dinner, Christine and Steve settled on the couch to watch a movie. But Christine kept glancing toward the stairs.

"What's wrong?" Steve asked. "You keep looking over there."

"I don't know," Christine replied, her voice uneasy. "I swear I hear voices upstairs."

Steve tilted his head, listening for a moment. "I don't hear anything. Want to go check on Jesse? I'm not that into this movie anyway."

Christine hesitated; her eyes fixed on the staircase. "Yeah. Let's go."

They tidied the living room, the sound of muffled voices growing louder as they ascended the stairs. Christine shot Steve a nervous glance.

"You hear it now, don't you?" she whispered.

Steve nodded; his voice tight. "Yeah… Maybe Jesse fell asleep watching TV in our room."

They made their way down the hall, but as they neared Jesse's door, it became clear that the noise wasn't coming from their bedroom. It was coming from his.

Christine slowly pushed open the door and staggered back, gagging as the foul stench hit her like a physical blow. It was the rancid smell of something decayed, a mix of bile and rot. She covered her mouth, but it was too late—her stomach lurched, and she rushed to the bathroom to vomit.

Steve gagged, too, his eyes watering as he pulled a handkerchief from his pocket, pressing it to his nose. He braved the stench and stepped inside the room.

When Christine returned, still pale, she stared in horror at the sight before her. The room was hot, unbearably so, but the walls were covered in a thin layer of ice, cracked and splintered. The air felt thick, suffocating, and the smell was even worse than before.

Jesse lay in bed, shirtless, his small body a sickly bluish hue. The blanket had been kicked down to the foot of the bed. His skin was covered in open sores, his face marred with deep gashes, some still oozing blood. His eyes were bloodshot, their edges pulled tight, giving him a strange, almost alien look. His teeth, once healthy, looked rotten, crumbling in his mouth. His shoulders were smeared with dried vomit.

Christine's heart shattered. This was her baby boy, but he looked like something monstrous. She moved closer, choking back her revulsion.

"Jesse?" she whispered, her voice trembling.

Jesse stirred, his eyes fluttering open. When he spoke, it was in a language she didn't understand, something guttural and foreign. Each word he spat brought a puff of dark, rancid smoke that filled the room with an even fouler stench. Christine recoiled but forced herself to step closer.

As his words became clearer, her maternal instinct kicked in, and she leaned forward to comfort him. Just as she reached out, his head snapped toward her, eyes blazing with something vicious.

With terrifying speed, he grabbed her hair and yanked her face close to his. "Bitch, this is all your fault," he hissed, his voice twisted with malice. "Because of you, I'm like this."

Christine froze, her heart racing in her chest. This wasn't her son. This was something else. Something dark.

Jesse tightened his grip, pulling her hair painfully. His voice dropped to a mocking whisper. "Tell your husband the truth. This is not his child."

Steve, standing at the doorway in stunned silence, could only stare as the words tore through the room like daggers.

Jesse turned his head toward Steve. "Remember that business trip to St. Louis, old man?" His voice dripped with venom. "That night your wife, this whore, invited men into your home. So many men… She let them take turns with her, over and over. This child you call yours isn't of your blood. You should've heard her squeal."

The words echoed like poison in the room. Jesse's laugh was cruel, a sound so dark it chilled Christine to the bone. He released her, and she stumbled backward, shock and shame overwhelming her.

Jesse collapsed onto the bed, writhing in pain, his words turning back to incoherent babbling.

"Steve…" Christine's voice was barely a whisper, her face wet with tears. "I don't know what that was. I swear, I've never seen anything like this."

Steve wrapped his arms around her, but his mind was spinning, unable to shake what Jesse had said. "It'll be okay," he whispered, though a seed of doubt had already taken root deep inside.

"Call Michelle. She's a doctor—she'll know what to do," Steve said, his voice distant. "Maybe she can help us. Or at least know someone who can."

Christine wiped her tears and hurried downstairs to call her sister, but Steve stayed, staring at Jesse, the weight of those words pressing down on him like a curse.

CHAPTER
FIVE

CHRISTINE HURRIED TO the door as soon as she heard the bell, she opened the door and saw Michelle Walker there on the porch Michelle stood before her, her simple frail figure clads in a black summer dress, which rested at mid-thigh. Her long blond hair fell smoothly over her tanned shoulders. Her blue-green eyes fluxed in gold dimmed as she saw the fear and worry in her sister's eyes. Christine smoothed her tangled hair.

"Hi, Christine," Michelle responded in a timid voice. "You sounded awful on the phone. What's going on?"

"You're not going to believe this. Come up to Jesse's room."

Christine hurried Michelle into the house and up the stairs. "What's wrong? Is Jesse hurt?"

"That's just it, Michelle. We don't know what's wrong with him."

She handed Michelle a small towel from the closet and grabbed one for herself as well. Trust me you're going to need it."

As they neared Jesse's room, Christine could once again hear the voices that she had heard before. Michelle looked at Christine as they both raised their towels to cover their mouths. Even in the hallway, the stench was overwhelming. As Christine opened the door, she was shocked to see Steve tying their son to the bed. Christine rushed toward the bed but her husband put his hand out to stop her. "Steve! What in the world are you doing to him?" Christine cried.

"Believe me. If I had any other choice, I wouldn't do this. I had to Christine. Please understand."

Steve bent over Jesse as if to check his temperature, and as he did, Jesse opened his mouth. Something large came out of his open mouth. The thing appeared to have a hand on the end of it and grabbed at his father's face. Steve pulled back as Jesse fought against the ties. It seemed as though he realized he was restrained and released his father. Steve stumbled back against the wall and Michelle put out her arms to steady him. Jesse's body arched upward as he growled at his captors. The massive blood-filled boils on his chest receded inward, leaving it smooth and tender. The child then screamed in torturous agony as blisters bubbled on his chest as if, he was being branded by some invisible force. They became so huge that some burst and leaked fluid down his side. Slowly, a upside-down pentagram began to take form. In an unconscious effort, Michelle moved toward the young boy to comfort him. As she reached the bed, she was assaulted by a voice so deep and heavy it caused her to stagger back. The voice continued to bark in many languages. The symbol on his chest began to recede once again and, in its place, Chinese calligraphy appeared.

"My God Michelle, I want my little boy back," Steve screamed. "I don't know who this is. I've never seen anything like this before but only in stupid movies. Please help us, help us please!"

"Unfortunately, Steve, I have seen something like this before." Michelle motioned the two to follow her. "Come downstairs and let me tell you about it." She motioned at Jesse. "You have him restrained tight enough. He'll be okay. Come on."

The three adults turned and went down the hall.

At the bottom of the stairs Steve headed away from the women and into the den. Michelle and Christine followed him. When they entered the den, they were surprised to see Steve in front of the open liquor cabinet. He pulled down three crystal bottles and set them on the bar. He looked at each one, as though trying to make a selection. Then he took a pitcher from the cabinet, poured the contents of the three decanters into it and began to drink. His hands shook so badly that the liquor began to spill on the floor. Michelle took the pitcher from him, poured him a small glass, and led him to a nearby chair.

"Just sit there and listen, Steve. I know you're upset but passing out won't help Jesse."

Michelle looked across the room and saw Christine sitting on the floor near the doorway, her knees pulled tight into her chest. Tears were running down her face and she was clutching Jesse's teddy bear. Michelle took a bottle of wine from the cabinet and poured a glass for Christine. She helped her sister to her feet and led her to the couch. Then she sat across from the two of them, a serious look on her face.

"It happened about eight years ago. Do you remember when I went to China on a mountain climbing expedition? You've seen the pictures from that trip, right Christine?"

CHAPTER

SIX

MT. EVEREST REGION EIGHT YEARS BEFORE

THE SKY WAS a beautiful turquoise as the twin engine plane made its final descent. Still jittery from the rough flight, Michelle subconsciously fidgeted with a small golden pendant. It was a token from a newly acquired boyfriend who was an up-and-coming martial arts champion. Before the pontoons of the plane touched down near the center of a calm lake, Michelle peered through the glass and saw a tiny snow-covered village on the north side of the icy lake.

"Jake. Is that where we're going? That little group of huts over there?" Michelle looked inquisitively at the pilot.

"Sure is," Jake replied. "Not exactly the Ritz Carlton, I know. But this village is known for its guides. I'm sure you won't be disappointed. Just hope you ladies weren't expecting to spend the evening in the spa. About the closest thing you'll get here is a swim in this lake."

"Well, Jake, comfort wasn't the selling point on this trip," Michelle laughed. "We're here for adventure. Right, ladies?" "That's right, Michelle," Pam scoffed.

Pam wasn't really thrilled about the mountain climbing expedition her best friend Michelle had planned. Pam was never into the whole physical activity thing. Her idea of a good workout was having to carry her own bags out of the shopping mall. "We could have stayed home and been pampered, but noooo. You wanted to go and conquer some god-forsaken mountain. This had better be good."

Michelle smiled at Pam. It had taken a lot of convincing to get her friend to come on this trip. Of all the other women in this group, Pam was the only one she hadn't managed to convince. Pam was still holding out for a spa in Palm Springs. "I promise, Pam, if you live through this, we'll go to Palm Springs for a week on me. Deal?"

Pam leaned forward and looked out at the dock in the distance. "Deal."

The plane taxied up and docked beside a long pier. Michelle, Pam, and the other women gathered their bags and exited the plane. Michelle walked down the pier toward a young Asian man. "Hi. I'm Michelle Walker. We're the expedition you've been expecting. I'm looking for our climbing guide."

The young man bowed slightly and then greeted Michelle with a handshake. "Hi, pleasure to meet you. I am Chun Choy," the young man replied. "You all can call me Lee. I will be your guide."

Michelle gave the man a rather doubtful glance. "Aren't you a little young to be a guide?"

Chun Choy looked at her with a disturbed glance. Apparently, she was as stupid and shallow as all the other American tourists who came here looking for adventure. "Aren't you a little soft to be a mountain climber?" he retorted.

Michelle was taken aback by his comment but she did understand his point. She smiled ruefully and blushed at her own idiocy. Just then she heard a noise and turned to look back down the pier. "Michelle? Soft?" Pam chimed in. "I hardly think so."

Pam stumbled up the pier behind Michelle. She was carrying at least five matching suitcases and was followed by the harried looking pilot with another four. "Michelle is the toughest woman I know. I think your mountain should be way more afraid of Michelle than she is of it."

She set down her bags with a thump. "Shit. Broke a nail, Michelle, you owe me a manicure."

Chun Choy looked a bit annoyed as Michelle tried to hurry the other women along. They gathered all their belongings and with a little help from some of the villagers, were soon on their way to their accommodations.

As they passed the center of the village, Michelle noticed a man sitting in front of a hut drawing blood from his arm with a knife and draining it into a bowl. She had never seen such a thing but didn't want to offend any of the villagers with her curiosity. She decided to ask Chun Choy about it later.

Many people waved and bowed to them as they walked toward the hut where they would be staying. Michelle noticed that everyone seemed to treat Chun Choy with great deference, as if he were a local celebrity of some sort. She wondered why he was held in such high esteem. Another question she would ask later.

At the far end of the village was a hut set a little way away from the rest of the other dwellings. It seemed somewhat larger than the others she had seen. Chun Choy pointed to it.

"Home sweet home, ladies", Chen Choy replied. "This is where you will be staying until we start our climb. I hope you find it comfortable and to your liking."

He opened the door to the hut and the women peered inside.

"This is a joke, right?" Pam said incredulously. "A hotel must be around here somewhere. There is no way I'm sleeping in there."

"I agree with Pam," stammered Lisa. Lisa was one of the first women who agreed to take the adventure with Michelle, but as she looked around, she began to regret her decision.

Just then, a rat ran from the hut and across Michelle's boot. She shuddered slightly but Pam screamed and hurled herself into Chun Choy's arms. He dropped all the suitcases as he tried to catch her.

"Ooh. Nice arms, Chang."

"It's Chun Choy, ma'am."

He sat her down on one of the small cots and picked up the suit-cases again. He quickly settled the women into their new home and then stepped outside the hut with Michelle.

"I'm sorry about Pam, Mr. Chun Choy. She can be a bit abrasive." Chun Choy gave her a small smile.

"It's okay. I'm used to it. Anything else I can help you ladies with for now?"

"Yeah. A couple of things." She turned toward Chun Choy with an inquisitive look.

"How come your name is Lee but everyone calls you Chun Choy?"

Michelle ran a hand through her golden tresses and gazed evenly at Chun Choy.

"Chun Choy is my nickname" Lee replied.

"What does it mean?"

"How can I translate this… it means short circuit, not all there, something missing upstairs."

He gave Michelle a wry grin as she lapsed into laughter.

"How very appropriate. You'd have to be crazy to make mountain climbing your profession, especially in this part of the world."

Chun Choy was a bit irritated with the way this American found humor in his nickname. He was very contented with his profession and didn't appreciate her taking it lightly. "We are a people of mountain climbers. I learned from my father who learned from his father. It has been passed from generation to generation as far back into time as we have lived here. I'm very proud of what I do and I am considered by my people to be the very best at what I do." "I was given this name by my Great Grandfather during my martial arts training years ago he was a Tibetan monk. I was nine years old and quick to fight anyone therefore I was given this name, it has nothing to do with mountain climbing."

Michelle was somewhat embarrassed and taken aback at his reply. She felt bad that she had appeared the conceited American tourist once again. "I'm sorry. I didn't mean to offend you."

"Forget about it. You just didn't understand."

He thought for a moment and said, "Get some rest. We start first thing in the morning. You'll need all your strength. The mountain air is not very forgiving from here on up.

CHAPTER

SEVEN

MICHELLE RETIRED TO her room. Pam grabbed a hold of her as she walked in. "You know, Michelle, I was really pissed when you landed that hunk of a boyfriend you have now, but if you plan to take the only good-looking guy in this freaken village as well, I may just have to kick your ass all the way up the mountain."

"What, Mr. Lee?" Michelle looked a bit puzzled. "No, don't worry. He's not my type. And besides, I think he has a crush on you."

Michelle knew this was a lie, but the smile it put on Pam's face was enough to shut her up. It might also make the mountain climb a bit more interesting.

The expedition began at sunrise, just as Chun Choy had promised. The walk up the mountain was not taxing for the first few hours. Michelle spent most of the walk snapping pictures of the breathtaking wonders that surrounded her. But as the sun set, the trail grew more treacherous and rugged. Dirt paths were replaced by rows of jagged rocks hidden by layers of ice and snow. Just before the sun dropped behind the peaks, a shrill cry broke the silence of the trek.

"AGGGHHH! Shit! I think I just broke my freaken leg!"

The group turned around to see Pam slumped to the ground grabbing her left leg and screaming in agony. Michelle ran to her friend who was struggling to free her foot from several rocks.

Michelle looked down and gasped. "Don't move, Pam. I hate to tell you this, but you were right. Your leg is broke."

Pam looked up at Michelle. "How can you tell? You haven't even touched my leg or anything"

Michelle held back a small chuckle as she turned to her friend. "I really don't have to feel for the bone, I'm staring at it right now, sticking through your pants."

Pam looked back at her leg. Blood had splattered all around the wound into the snow. The bright red stood out against the pure white as her focused turned toward the huge bone piercing out from her pant leg. Pam grew dizzy as she looked at the hideous wound. Lisa ran up to Pam and held her to prevent her from falling as she passed out.

"Someone locate me some sticks," Michelle called out to the group. "About two feet long, and an inch in diameter if possible." "I need to set this wound before we move her back down the mountain."

Although she had never worked on a friend before, this was not the most grotesque thing she had seen. Michelle had struggled through medical school as well as her residency at County Hospital. Because of her modelesque looks, no one, not even her professors, took her seriously as a doctor. Although most of them took her seriously as a love interest, just some fling their wives should never find out about. But Michelle was a hell of a lot smarter than all of them gave her credit for, graduating with honors at the top of her class. Even this success had given her a reputation for sleeping with her professors to get the grades. She couldn't win for losing. But she didn't care. She fought for every test score and every honor she received. In the end, she knew she was that damn good and no one could take it away from her.

Chun Choy had grabbed two sticks just as she described. As she set the sticks next to Pam's leg, she unwrapped her scarf from her neck. The gold medallion she wore was stuck to the scarf. As she pulled the scarf from her neck, the medallion fell to the ground. Chun Choy rushed forward to collect the medallion from the blood-covered snow. As he polished it off, he noticed the symbol etched into the gold coin. He knew now was not the time to ask about it and decided to file the question away until they returned to the village and knew the fallen woman would be okay.

Michelle looked up at Pam's face as Pam began to come to. Not a good time for her to regain consciousness Michelle thought to herself. She glared deeply into Pam's eyes. "Pam, this is going to hurt a little... well actually it's going to hurt a hell of a lot." Michelle held back another chuckle as she realized the irony of the moment. The one woman on the trip who really didn't want to be there was down, bleeding all over the newly fallen snow.

Pam stared at her friend as Michelle signaled Chun Choy and Lisa to restrain Pam. She grabbed a hold of Pam's leg just above and below the fracture. "Are you ready, we'll go on three. One... Two..."

"Wait!" yelled Pam. "Hold on a sec. Lisa get me my backpack."

Lisa pulled off Pam's pack. "Now reach in the side pocket and give me the flask."

Lisa pulled out the small flask and stared at it with a puzzled look. Michelle too seemed startled by the request and the flask.

"What is that?" asked Michelle with a frustrated tone.

"It's bourbon," Pam smiled. "I brought it just in case of an emergency. And I figure this is an emergency."

Michelle grabbed the flask. She poured a bit of it on the wound then gave the flask to Pam. "Drink this, you'll need it."

"No shit, Sherlock." Pam grabbed the flask and killed the rest of the contents. "Okay," Michelle said, "are you ready? On three."

Pam held the flask tight to her chest, gritting her teeth. "Okay, on three."

"Okay, here we go…. one…."

Before Michelle counted two, she grabbed a hold of her friend's leg and pulled the sides apart as hard as she could, setting the bone back together under the skin.

"SHIIIIIIIIIT" Pam cried out. "What the hell happened to two! You did that on purpose, you jealous bitch!"

Michelle starred at her friend calmly. "I told you it was going to hurt like hell."

"Bullshit!" Pam screamed. "You did that on purpose because Chang here likes me and not you!"

"It's Chun Choy," Michelle laughed, "and you had better just calm down so we can get you down the mountain."

As Pam slid back into unconsciousness, Chun Choy brought over a small stretcher he had the ladies put together while Michelle set the leg. "Here, we can carry her down on this." "It's good and strong"

Michelle and Chun Choy placed Pam on the stretcher and wrapped her in several blankets. "We must not try to head back down the trail tonight," Chun Choy stated. "We should camp here for the night and head back at dawn."

The night dragged by, the sun seemingly taking forever to rise again. As the sun finally peeked over the mountain stops, the mountain winds blew the morning haze out of camp. The sun now able to shine through the clouds pointed out the path home back to the village. Nearly half the day went by before they reached the village. Pam was rushed into the village clinic where her wound was cleaned and treated. After dropping her pack off at the hut, Michelle went to visit her friend.

"How are you feeling?" she asked.

"There you go again, you and your dumb ass questions," Pam scolded. "I have just seen my own leg bone sticking through my skin and you ask how I'm feeling? For a doctor, you sure are stupid."

"I'm glad to see you back to your normal self," Michelle laughed. "I'll check back on you in a little while. For now, get some sleep." Pam quickly grabs Michelle's arm.

"Michelle thanks… for saving me and what not."

Michelle looked at her friend with a smile then left the make shift clinic. As she walked out the clinic door, Chun Choy rushed up to her. "I really have to say you amazed me up there. I have not met many women who could keep their composure like that looking at what we saw."

"It's my job to see things like that," replied Michelle.

"Well regardless, I just wanted to say I am impressed by you. And I wanted to ask about your pendent. Do you know what the symbols mean?"

Michelle looked down at her neck. She hadn't realized that her necklace was missing. "My necklace! It must have fallen off during the commotion."

Chun Choy held out his hand, revealing the medallion he had recovered from the snow. "Here, it fell off when you removed your scarf for the splint. That's when I saw the marking."

"Thank you, but to answer your questions, no, I do not know what they mean."

Michelle took the medallion and placed it back on her neck. She held it in her hand and stared at the symbol, noticing for the first time it was there.

"The symbol translates roughly to 'bearer of light'," Chun Choy replied. "Basically, it means someone who is true to themselves and others, trustworthy. Something like that. Pretty hard to translate into English." "It is in our old Tibetan language. I possess one as well."

Michelle again stared at her medallion. She had remembered her boyfriend mentioning something about it, but hadn't given much thought to it until now.

"How would you like to see a ceremony that no outsider has ever witnessed before?" Chun Choy asked.

"What kind of ceremony?" Michelle was interested to learn all she could about this man and his culture.

"You'll see. I'll explain everything tonight," Chun Choy replied. "I'll come get you after dinner."

With that, he turned and walked away.

EIGHT

MICHELLE WENT BACK inside the hut and finished unpacking. She wondered at just what sort of ceremony she would see. Everything was so different here. Anything could happen. Just after sunset, Chun Choy arrived to collect Michelle for the evening's events. She was still unnerved by the details he had thus far given her.

"What kind of ceremony is it?" Michelle asked. "And why would you invite a complete stranger to something so sacred. It just doesn't make sense."

Chun Choy looked at her and smiled an awkward smile. "First of all, it's not quite a ceremony, really. It's more like a sacrifice. And secondly, you're invited because of the pendant you wear on your neck. Only certain people wear such things."

"It's not really mine. I got this from my boyfriend who received it from his martial arts master while he lay on his death bed."

"Well let me tell you. That symbol not only represents truth, but also power.

Actually, it represents the ultimate power. Do you know what that is? True love." "You're talking about truth and love and we are going to see a sacrifice?"

Michelle's stomach turned over. She had heard of such things but had never thought about witnessing such a ritual. Michelle stopped in her tracks.

"You're kidding, right? This is all some kind of weird initiation for mountain climbers, right?" Chun Choy replied, "Maybe this was a bad idea on my part" "you are obviously not ready for this, I apologize to you and will take you back to your quarters" But it was too late Michelle curiosity had now gotten the better of her. "No, it's too late now she retorted, you have proverbially let the cat out of the bag, and I want to know more!" "So, answer my questions"

"It's not a sacrifice in the Western sense," Chen Choy answered, trying to calm her down. "We do not just sacrifice an innocent victim. What it is… is a fight to the death. Each warrior is given a chance for survival." "Why do your people do this?" she asked.

"There is a child in the village with a "Kuei," Chun Choy replied.

"What the hell is a 'Kuei'?" Michelle had never heard the term before and was frankly very curious.

"Oh, I'm sorry," Chen Choy stated. A Kuei, as my people call it, is a demon."

Michelle was a little aggravated by the diagnosis. "A demon? There are no such things. Take me to the child. I have medical background. Maybe I can help. You don't have to go through with this." Michelle pleaded.

Then, in a sad voice, Chun Choy replied, "Five years ago the 'Kuei' went into a little boy. He would have been eleven years old next month."

He saw the unspoken question in Michelle's eyes. "Yes, he was my only son."

Chun Choy paused and looked out over the moonlit lake. "You see, I've been to your schools. I graduated from U.C.L.A. I once believed in your Western medicine. When I was in America I rejected the beliefs of my people. I felt that they were old fashioned and foolishly out of touch with modern society. I had a European doctor come and see my son and there wasn't a goddamn thing he could do."

Chun Choy stopped for a moment and turned away. Michelle could see the tension in him as he fought for control of his emotions. "Now I believe in the old ways."

He turned toward her and she was momentarily frightened by the anger in his eyes. "Soon, you will believe too. Are you absolutely sure you want to see this?" Michelle replied "yes" "Come let's go."

He held out his hand and she took it. "The ceremony starts soon. When it is over, I will take you to the child."

As Chun Choy escorted Michelle into the ceremonial area, she saw a large group of men seated in a circle. Oil torches dimly lit the area. Two men were sitting on opposite sides of the circle. One of the men from the outer circle handed a crude clay bowl to each man. Chun Choy leaned over and whispered to Michelle.

"It is a ritual among our people to consume blood before a fight to the death. You see, in ancient times, if a warrior knew that he might die in battle he would prepare himself through this ritual. He would request a family member, preferably someone young, would give a small amount of their blood. The warrior would then heat the blood slightly and consume it. Or the small person would be scared so the blood would be more potent. Your western medicine calls it "Adrenochrome". It comes from the adrenal glands in the body, when the flight or fight response is triggered in the brain, the adrenalin gets dupped into the blood stream. That's why there needs to be a battle. The warrior would gain a feeling of great strength from this, almost a drugged state. You know, like how you think you can fly or knock down a brick wall with your bare hands. Stuff like that."

Michelle nodded in understanding, and then glanced back at the two men. What she had seen in the village the other day must somehow be related to the ceremony that unfolded before her. The men were lifting the bowls to their mouths. She shuddered as she saw a stream of human blood trickle down one warrior's cheek.

Chun Choy's face grew solemn. "There are consequences to this though. It can really mess with the warrior's head. Make him feel like shit for a couple of days after the effect wears off."

The men stood and faced off. Michelle leaned closer to Chun Choy. "You said that in ancient times it was a family member who would give the blood. Was it also, a family member that fought for a life? Did you fight for your son?"

"No. I never had a chance to fight for my son. It was a hard lesson to learn and one I will not soon forget. The elders told me how important it was but I was too blind by modern ways and too stubborn to listen to them. It will never happen to me or to a member of my village again. Not if I have anything to do with the matter."

He looked out at the two men again. A look of sorrow crossed his even features. "These men are brothers. The younger one saved the older one's life when they were small boys. They had been playing near the edge of a cliff near the path we walked up yesterday. It had been raining earlier in the day and the older boy slipped in the mud and fell over the edge, barely managing to grab several roots that had been uncovered by the rain. The younger boy, knowing he had not the time to get help, pulled the belt out of his pants, grabbed onto a nearby branch and lowered the belt to his brother. We are not sure where he got the strength to pull his brother up for the cliff, but the two have been inseparable ever since. They have always been very close. It is sad that tonight one of them will take the life of the other. The older man is the girl's father and the younger man is her uncle."

"Brothers?" asked Michelle. "How could they stand to fight each other? I would think that such a thing would be impossible."

"I don't think you understand the point of this, Michelle. They have no choice but to fight each other. It isn't a vicious thing, or even a violent thing. It is just something they must do to save the child."

Michelle grew angry after hearing such a tale. "You're right. I don't understand. I don't even think I want to watch. But I can tell you want me to see this. Just don't expect me to enjoy it."

"I don't. And I appreciate you staying. Listen, this will be over in just a few moments. The men are ready now."

Michelle sat back and watched. The two men circled each other cautiously. Each of them held a knife in one hand and kept the other hand slightly extended, seemingly for balance. As if on cue, they ran toward each other at full speed. The sparks flew as their blades clashed against each other. With a crushing blow, the two men made contact. The girl's father moved so fast that Michelle was unable to see what was happening for a moment. Then she saw that he had his brother in a painful arm lock. The daughter's father held the knife to his brother's chest but hesitated. Michelle could see the agony in his eyes and wondered how he could bring himself to complete the job at hand. The little girl's uncle sensed that his brother could not force himself to do harm to his own brother. Michelle watched as the uncle took it upon himself and plunged the gleaming steel deep into his own chest. His heart exploded with the force of the blow and he died instantly, crumpling to the ground at his brother's feet. His brother dropped to his knees and pulled him into his arms. Tears began to flow down Michelle's cheeks as she watched the man hold his brother. The child's father screamed in agony over the horror of his brother's death. Blood covered his hands and seeped into the earth. The men that had been seated in the circle came forward to help the little girl's father. They laid the brother on the ground and quickly sliced his neck through to the spine. The head was bent aside and a bowl was held to the open neck to catch the remaining blood.

Michelle stood quickly, her head spun and she felt herself start to retch. "Get me the fuck out of here." She requested.

She held her stomach until the feeling passed. Her legs felt weak and immovable. She turned and walked as fast as she could away from the circle. She saw a hut nearby and stumbled up to it, pressing her hands against the walls for support. She sobbed quietly as she stood there. After a moment, she felt a hand on her back and she stiffened.

"It's just me." Chun Choy replied. "I'm so sorry. I believe it may have affected you more than I realized. Are you going to be alright?"

"I doubt it. That was the most awful thing I have ever seen. Now what happens? Is this little girl suddenly cured... what could make this all seem worthwhile?"

"Do you want to go see the little girl? I think it would help you understand."

Michelle objected for a moment but then nodded in agreement. She followed Chun Choy to the far side of the village where the little girl and her family lived.

When they came near to the small dwelling, Michelle noticed a pungent smell in the air. She wrinkled her nose in disgust as Chun Choy motioned her inside.

The child lay on a small bed of bamboo. Her mother hovered at her side trying to comfort her child. She dipped a clean cloth into a bowl of water at the bedside and gently rubbed it across the child's forehead and neck. Michelle noticed that the little girl's color was bad, as if she were jaundiced. Her eyes were bloodshot and swollen, the veins prominent. The pupils of her eyes sparkled in the lamplight and Michelle was shocked to see that they were not the dark brown of oriental eyes but a brilliant green almost that of new oak leaves. The child rubbed at her arms and Michelle noticed that she was covered with bloody, oozing sores. Her skin seemed terribly scarred as if she had been horribly burned. As Michelle watched the tiny girl suffer in silence, she noticed that the child's arms and legs had been tied to the four corners of the bed with a thick rope. She leaned over to Chun Choy and whispered in his ear.

"Why in the world did they tie her down? She's practically a baby!"

Chun Choy placed his hand on Michelle's shoulder. "She is very strong and cannot be trusted. She has a child demon in her. The demon spawn are not strong enough to feed on adults, so they victimize our children."

Just then, the little girl looked straight into Michelle's eyes. Michelle began to see disturbing things in her mind's eye. Things like gang violence beyond any experienced before, and horrible, gruesome things like cannibalism. She shook her head and tried to remove the images. Instead of becoming fainter they seemed to intensify. Michelle watched helplessly as an enormous meteor plummeted to the earth, destroying the planet and ending all life as we know it. She stumbled back against the doorway as the vision finally faded.

Chun Choy rushed to Michelle's side to steady her. "What is it, Michelle? What did you see?"

She leaned on the frame of the doorway, a hopeless look on her face. "I... I'm not sure what I saw. I think it was the future. I'm not sure. All I know is that it was violent and awful and terrifying."

"The demon plays tricks with your mind," Chun Choy revealed in a reassuring voice. "It takes from within you what you fear most. Don't believe anything that you have seen. Others have had visions in the presence of the demon. They are meant only to frighten you, giving the demon more power"

Michelle eased away from the door and walked toward the little girl on the bed.

"You were right before, Chun Choy. There is nothing I can do for her. My medical talents have no power over this kind of sickness. Poor little angel."

She leaned toward the little girl and held out her hand to stroke her brow. The little girl smiled sweetly, and then her expression changed. Her eyes began to glow with a great intensity and strange noises came from her throat. Michelle tried to step back from the bed but was not quick enough. The child vomited violently, covering the sheets of the bed as well as Michelle's blouse. Her mother rushed forward to change the sheets and clean the child as Michelle and Chun Choy made a rather quick exit from the small home.

As they walked toward the hut where Michelle and the other women were staying, Chun Choy tried to help Michelle make sense of the events of the day.

"I've never seen anything like this before, Chun Choy. I've traveled all over the world and I truly thought I'd seen most everything. I guess I was wrong."

"No one knows everything, Michelle. Any wise person can tell you that." He turned away from Michelle's lodging and headed toward the center of town again.

"Where are you going?"

"To see the offering. It is the most important part. You coming?"

"Not like this, I'm not. I'll be right back."

Michelle ran inside her hut and changed quickly. On her bed was a note from Pam.

"Michelle honey, I and the other girls went to a nearby hot spring. The doctor said it would be fine as long as I kept my leg out of the water. I guess there are some benefits to coming on this trip. I'm sure glad I brought several bottles of my good bourbon. Anyway, when you're done with that fine looking guide of yours, send him my way. With my leg and all, I can sure use him after a few drinks! Ha! Ha! We will be back in a few hours. Love, Pam."

When she came back outside, she saw that Chun Choy had gone. She seen him at the far end of the street and ran to catch up with him.

"Wait! I'm coming!" She caught up with him in a few moments. Breathless, she asked, "Why do they have to kill a person to get the blood? Won't any blood do? I mean, why not a sheep or goat or something? I mean, they could even get the men of the village to donate a pint or something. Families do that all the time in the States."

Chun Choy shook his head. "Believe me, we've tried that. It was like giving the demon something that left a bad taste in its mouth. The demon gets very angry. It is an awful thing."

"How can you tell the demon is angry? Does it start to throw things or something?" "What?"

"No, much worse. It sends the child's soul away to the dwelling place of the beast. Then it mutilates the child's body for all to see."

"Oh! crap! I can see now why you feel this is the only recourse." Michelle looked up at Chun Choy with a puzzled glare. "But tell me, how does the demon communicate? Is it different with each possession?"

"No. It is pretty much the same each time. Did you see the markings on the little girl's chest?"

Michelle nodded yes. "There is a reason for those markings. The demon is using the girl's body as a canvas for its demands. The reason you didn't recognize the markings is that they are in ancient Chinese, Tibetan language. Local legend has it that there is a demon that will play with its victim until the soul is fully awake. Then it kills the victim by decapitation. Killing in this manner allows the heart to continue pumping briefly. This helps the demon to consume the victim's soul."

Michelle looked at her guide with a doubting look. "You have got to be kidding, that is the most hideous thing I've ever heard."

Chun Choy put his hands on Michelle's shoulders. "Why in the world would I kid about something like this, Michelle? If I was going to initiate you, I'd put itching powder in your bed, or something stupid like that, not mutilate a child.

Get a grip. This is real and it's horrible and it is scary. But is it the truth."

Michelle started to weep again. "I never cry and it seems that I have been doing nothing but cry since I got to this god-forsaken place." She sat down heavily in the dirt of the street.

"Go on. I can't handle any more. I've had it. I want to go home."

Chun Choy reached down and pulled Michelle up. "Come with me, I haven't known you very long but I can tell you're not a quitter. Let's go." They walked in silence for a while.

Michelle wiped the tears from her eyes. "You told me that the demon wants the soul to be fully awake. Just what does that mean?"

"Fully awake? I'm not completely sure but that is the term that is always used. In my medical opinion, I believe that the demon is after the chemicals produced in the body. You know, the runner's high. The feeling of elation you get when you are working out really hard or making love. Endorphins, they call them. That is why there must be a sacrifice. The victim is so terrified that the endorphin count in the blood is at its highest. It makes the demon strong."

They had walked the length of the village and now came to a clearing on the edge of town. In the center of the clearing was a huge marble statue of some ancient god that Michelle didn't recognize.

Chun Choy slowed down as they entered the clearing. "This is where the villagers worship. You have seen that we have a Buddhist temple and a Christian church, but nearly all of the villagers still live by many of the old ways. See the small platform in front? Watch what will happen."

The men from the fight were gathered around the small clearing in straight rows. One man took the bowl of blood that had been taken from the child's uncle and set it on the platform. Michelle seen smoke coming from the statue and smelled a sweet odor in the air.

"Incense. It sharpens the senses," replied Chun Choy.

There was a small fire on the platform and after a few moments it looked as though the blood was beginning to boil. Michelle looked up and seen that the eyes of the statue had begun to glow. Blood ran from both the eyes and the ears of the statue. Michelle heard a scream from behind her and looked at Chun Choy.

"It's the little girl. The demon is leaving her. Come quickly. I'll show you."

They hurried back to the girl's home. As they got closer Michelle noticed that the smell was gone. The little girl's mother came out of the house and spoke to Chun Choy.

"She says that her daughter is resting comfortably now. The demon seems to be gone. The scream we heard when we were in the clearing was that of little girl. She began to have convulsions and large bumps developed on her chest. They began to move upward toward her head. That is when she screamed. Her throat swelled so much that her mother thought it would burst. Then her head swelled for a moment as the demon left through her mouth. Now she is sleeping and seems to be all right. She is a very lucky child. Lucky to have a family who is willing to give up their lives to save hers Michelle replied. She will have little to no memory of what she has been through, but the scars will be there forever."

CHAPTER
NINE

PRESENT DAY NEW YORK

MICHELLE STOOD UP from the couch and paced across the room. She looked out the window at the sun that was just peeking over the trees to the east.

"I don't know if it's the same thing that's happening to Jesse or not. But you have to admit that the similarities are pretty scary. You know I'll do everything I can to help. Listen, I need to do some research. If there are any changes in Jesse's condition, please call me."

"Thanks Michelle. We'll be fine. Or at least as good as we can be in this situation. I'm going upstairs and stay by Jesse."

Christine left the room and headed upstairs. Steve stood and walked Michelle to the door. "Thanks for your help, Michelle. Tell me honestly. Is he going to be all right?"

Michelle looked at her brother-in-law. "I don't know, Steve. I really don't. We may very well be able to save him. Then again, we may not. What I really need from you right now is your strength. You need to stay calm for your wife and child. Try not to let this throw you. I know it's awful, but we will make it through this somehow. "That much I can promise you."

Michelle hugged him warmly and hurried down the steps to her car.

✳   ✳   ✳

Joe walked into his house and heard the familiar beep of the answering machine. As he tossed his keys into a nearby ashtray, he hit the playback button.

"Hi honey, it's Michelle. Listen, I need to work late tonight so I'm afraid I'll need to take a rain check on that dinner you promised me. I'm really sorry, but there is something wrong with Jesse, my nephew. If you need me, I'll have the cell phone on. Love you… bye."

"Shit. She would have to cancel tonight." Joe said to himself.

Joe grabbed his keys and his portfolio of exercises for his afternoon karate class. "And what in the world does Jesse have to do with her working late? I guess she'll tell me tonight."

He slammed the door behind him as he went down the steps. An hour later, Joe's class was well underway. He asked one of his students to step forward. "James, come to the front of the class please."

James walked over to Joe and stood there. Joe paced the front of the class for a moment. "James, here's a situation for you: a man, obviously drunk, walks up to you on a street corner and says 'Hey Mr. Tough guy! I'm going to kick the crap out of you.' What would you do?"

A very cocky James answered, "I'd hit the jerk so hard that his teeth would come out of his butt in single file."

All the students started to laugh. Joe looked at his student, amused by his response. "Okay, did everyone hear that? Sounds good right? But here's the problem. You're going to hit a complete stranger in the mouth, right? In the process of my teeth leaving my gums, they cut your knuckles and I bleed all over your hand and I have AIDS or some other infectious disease. What did you just do to yourself?"

The laughter stopped, as Joe's students suddenly found the moment not so funny anymore.

"Crap" James replied. "I didn't even think of that."

Joe continued to explain the consequences of fighting. "You all must remember, fighting is not all about how strong your body is, but how sharp your mind is as well. The two must work together if you are to truly master what I teach you."

After class, Joe went to his office and sat down. A knock on the wall next to the door broke the silence of his solitude. Joe looked up to see who it was. The door was open and James stood there with a smile.

"Come in, come in" Joe replied.

James walked in and sat down. James looked at his master who seemed a little distant.

"What's wrong?" he asked.

With a deep sigh, Joe looked up at his student. "You know me pretty well don't you! How many years have I known you, James?"

"I don't know, ten maybe?" James replied. "Why do you ask?"

Joe sat there silent, not saying a word, simply staring sternly into the eyes of his star pupil.

James, feeling the disappointment, lowered his head in shame. "I'm sorry for my remarks in class, Sensei. I just don't like the idea of people messing with me. Joe, you've been like a father to me, even after I tried to rob you like the stupid punk I was, and you stopped me. I know you could have hurt me bad but you didn't. You gave me a chance by taking me off the streets. I can't remember my parents; just how cold and scared and hungry I was. You taught me how to fight and gave me confidence and pride I had never had before. But most of all, you taught me how to love myself. So, you must understand the last thing I would ever want to do is offend you or what you have taught me."

The stern glare in Joe's eyes gave way to a smile. "Well, you know James, being a child wasn't the greatest of times for me either. I remember when my father would come home with his breath smelling bad. Every time he had this bad breath, he was always angry and would beat me and my mother. For years I thought that everybody who got mad would have this bad breath. I thought 'how neat, I can always tell when someone is mad.' How stupid of me! Anyway, when I was six years old, I experienced the worst Christmas I'd ever had. My father came home late and with his breath smelling worse than ever. He started beating my mother really bad. I tried to help my mom but my father backhanded me in the face, sending me into the Christmas tree. I saw my mother fall to the floor. My father grabbed a carpenter's hammer that she was using to hang Christmas stockings up and beat her with it. I know she died right there. I could see my mother's eyes as the life left her; my dad continued to beat her. He went to prison after that and I went to live with my grandmother. She's great. She always seemed to know what was bothering me. One time I came home from school and my grandmother already knew what had happened. She cleaned me up and then took me to my first martial arts class."

"As I started to learn, I took every chance I could to try out my new skills. I figured I'd show everyone how tough I was before they started picking on me. In a sense, I became the bully I was trying to defend myself against. My master pulled me off to the side one day. He asked why I fought so much. When I told him the reason, he challenged me to a fight right then and there. I wasn't sure why at the time, but I squared up and attacked. He beat the living hell out of me that day. As I lay there on the floor, he picked me up and gave me the most important lesson in my life. 'In the real world, you never know what dangers you will be facing. You don't know what others know. If you continue to rush into situations, I would find myself in worse shape than you are in now.' It was then that I realized it is better to try and get out of situations without fighting, than rushing in fists a blazing."

"At that moment, I made a promise to myself that when I became good enough, I would help others who could not help themselves. I did just that! You see, you have to realize that fighting is not always the best answer. You need to control your anger or you may end up a bloody mess in some back alley. Do you understand what I'm saying?"

The boy looked up at Joe and sighed. "Yes, sir. I promise I will work on controlling my temper."

Joe smiled. "Good. Well enough of that. Today is my grandmother's birthday and I got her a new cane, hand crafted, solid oak! Look at this... just underneath the handle is a button. Press it and wah lah... a razor-sharp handmade sword.

It's feather light. I hope she likes it." James nodded his head in agreement.

Joe continued, "She has an old cane. Had it ever since I can remember! The cane is very unusual. It has what looks like a Dragons Claw with its nails slightly embedded into a beautiful crystal stone. And get this! The crystal changes color when touched! I remember one time when I had some friends over to spend the night. I was very young then and my grandmother would entertain us kids. She would have all of us gather around her and she'd tell great stories. Then she would tell us what kind of person we were going to be. I can remember one boy named Billy. Now Billy was very hard headed and liked to bully all of us kids. My grandmother had Billy touch the crystal on her cane and it turned brown. A look of curiosity came over Billy's face as my grandmother told him that he was a bad and angry young man. She told him he had better stop killing small animals and bullying these young men because if he did not, his life here on earth would be very short lived. She emphasized that it wasn't too late. If the crystal had gone black, then it would have been too late! He still had a chance. 'Don't pass it up!' she told him. From that day on, Billy changed completely. "James, do you still go to that church down the street?" James nodded his head yes.

"Then you know Father McNelly, right?"

"Yes" James replied. "Father Billy McNelly? That was him?" He started to laugh.

Joe laughed as well "Yes that was him."

Joe then looked at his watch. "I need to go see my grandmother. I'll teach your next class. Not to worry." James stated.

Joe grabbed his gift and took off.

TEN

JOE PULLED UP to a beautiful house. It was a restored Victorian home with a wood porch full of plants and a wooden porch swing. The different color butterflies that circled the house when Joe was a boy were still there. He could always remember different kinds of life making their dwelling near their home. When Joe walked into his grandmother's house, the sweet smell of apple cinnamon pie flooded his nose, awakening memories and feelings of a time long gone.

Joe knocked on a door by the living room and walked into the room to see his grandmother sitting in a rocking chair. The sunlight was peeking through a large window in the living room, dancing off her shoulders. For a moment, it appeared as if a halo rested over her angelic head. Joe turned to close the door, and, when he looked back, the halo was gone. His grandmother looked up to see her pride and joy.

"Joe!" she replied. "Mihito! You have come to visit me!"

"Hi, Grandma. Yes, I came to see my favorite lady!"

"Come. Let me look at you. She stated. Ah! You are as handsome as ever!"

"Thank you, Grandma!" Joe's face lit up. "And you are as radiant as the morning sunshine. Here, Grandma. Look what I got you for your birthday!!"

Joe held the cane up for his grandmother's inspection. She took it in her hands, fingering the fine engravings on the end. "Thank you, my boy," she replied. "Come here and give me a hug."

Joe leaned over to hug her. She accepted the warm embrace and gently grabbed his upper arm. As she took hold of his arm, reality gave way to a nightmarish vision entering her mind. In her mind's eye, she saw a flash so bright, it caused her eyes to roll back and lips to fold into her mouth. Her grip tightened on his arm, causing his limb to go numb. The visions she had were quick flashes of the demon Celesthargor, Satan's general of his army of darkness. The killer of Stars/Angels from Heaven. This creature stood ten feet tall with four very muscular arms that moved along its body like serpents. Razor sharp cartilage scimitars protruded out of the inner side of its forearms giving the beast complete advantage over its prey. Its four powerful legs gave Celesthargor incredible balance and ability to climb any type of wall with great speed and agility. She saw it's thick, bulging crescent shaped eyes look directly at her. Another flash passed violently before her and again she sees the dark beast. This time it transforms within a victim. She sees it squeezing out of its victim's body like its being reborn. The body starts to split in half as a large amount of wet viscera slaps the cold concrete floor. The last flash she has is of Joe and Celesthargor. Joe is covered in blood, thrown up against a red brick wall in a dark alley with a dim street lamp shimmering down over him and the imp. She sees the demon about to destroy her grandson as the premonition ends. She snaps out of her vision and looks at Joe. In complete hysteria she says, "Joe, O my God it's time for me to go." "What?" Joe replied.

She continued to repeat:

"It's come." "I have to go!! I have to go. It's time for me! Celesthargor, is here! Celesthargor. "It's time. It's time."

Joe embraced his grandmother, trying to calm her from her frantic trance. "Oh my God!! What's wrong, Grandma, what's wrong?"

Joe stumbled around looking for her medication. He grabbed her purse, dumping the contents onto a nearby table. He tore open the small bottle, pouring the pills into his hand. He placed two into his grandmother's mouth and helped her wash them down with a glass of water. Within minutes, she began to relax, easing into her chair, exhausted from her ordeal. Joe gently lifted her out of the rocking chair and carried her down the hall into her bedroom. He gently put her in bed and tried to make her as comfortable as possible by fluffing the pillows. Fearing the worst, he stayed the night, canceling any plans that he may have had for the evening.

About 2:06 a.m. Joe woke abruptly, feeling as though something bad had happened. Clamoring to his feet, he hurried to his grandmother's room. There he discovered her motionless form slightly illuminated by the soft glow of a nearby house light that had filtered through the linen curtains, which draped the bedroom window.

Joe could only voice a small whisper. "Grandma?... Grandma?"

There was no answer. Joe rushed to her bedside, grabbing her lifeless hand. Joe's heart started to pound very deep within his chest. He knew what had happened but did not want to believe it. "Grandma, why? Why did you go?"

Joe started to cry as he sat down at the edge of her bed. He gently slipped his hands underneath her back and lifted her to him. As her head fell back, Joe placed his head at her chest and moaned a deep, painful cry. "Why, why did you leave me," he thought to himself. "It wasn't time yet. Why? Why did you leave me all alone?"

ELEVEN

MADAGASCAR—MAHAJANGA TWO WEEKS EARLIER

HEY! HEY! WHAT the hell are you doing? Dave Forest spouted. "The well needs to be a few more yards to the left. Can't you idiots read a damn map?"

Still yelling at the workers with the blueprints in hand with the Foreman at his side, he complains, "I'm only here for a few months and I'm here with a bunch of clowns".

The foreman responds, "Sorry Dave, but this is all we got, a bunch of underpaid, overworked villagers."

Dave agrees and continues, "the U.N. sent me over here to complete this irrigation job in only three freaken months and they expect me to complete it, I don't think so. I don't even want to be here."

The foreman in a hurry to leave, feels the bad vibes from Dave and responds, "Aaa, ya, I'll check on you later."

Dave Forest stood at the edge of the trench, and spotted a shimmering object in the mud. He signaled to a rig operator to stop digging and climbed down the twelve-foot trench. He pulled from the ground a decanter covered in mud. Cleaning it off, he noticed a beautiful turquoise center. He placed it in a coat pocket, and decided to wait to examine later.

That evening with caution and excitement, Dave pulled out the very valuable looking artifact. He looked at the dragon's head and the strange writings that adorned it, the crystal began to come apart, like a Chinese puzzle box. A flash of light slapped his face leaving him paralyzed. A few hours later a villager seeking Dave's assistance stumbled across him, apparently unconscious, but still standing, holding the strange artifact. The crystal container was separated into several pieces losing the radiant turquoise color.

Over the next several days Dave found himself exhausted, wanting only to sleep every minute. Several days later Dave was in his tent washing his face in front of the mirror, as he looked up into the mirror, he saw his reflection and for the first time he sees P'an Ku (The Angel) in the reflection but to everyone else they still saw Dave Forest.

By the third day after the incident, Dave finally dragged himself to work. He lost his train of thought randomly, finding it very hard to concentrate on any task. When Dave spoke to the villagers, he began to speak in an ancient Chinese tongue none of the villagers had heard. They had a hard time understanding him and began to worry about his health. Rumors filled the village that he had somehow become possessed.

As Dave stood beside a tree near a river, he saw something out of the corner of his eye. With an uncontrollable urge, his hand shot out in a blur, catching a water bug that flew from the tree. Pinching it between his fingers, he slipped it into his mouth. Before some unconscious part of his brain realized what he had done, the insect is ground into paste, bits of its shell stuck between his teeth.

The other U.N. members and villagers were transfixed on Dave's bizarre behavior. One of the villagers assisted him to his tent.

Later that night he was spotted in a clearing completely nude, on his knees with a small fire in front of him. His hands were stretched out to the heavens, speaking in the strange tongue he had recently picked up. A passing foreman spotted him in the field and quickly rounded up the other U.N. members to witness what was taking place. His U.N. partner reported him to their superior. In a frightening display of circumventing the bureaucratic red tape, Dave was packed for the nearest city and given a psychiatric evaluation. Opinions ranged from confused to mentally disturbed, but all suggested that Dave be relieved of his current field assignment. By the end of the week, he was on a plane back to his home in New York, no one realizing the existence of the entity that possessed him.

*　*　*

A few days before the death of Joe's grandmother, Dave Forest arrived at the John F. Kennedy International Airport, greeted by his family with a warm reception. He walked out of the airport lobby and stopped near the street curb. There he looked to his right and frowned as if he had tasted something bitter. "It's here," he thought to himself. But there was something different about the premonition he got from the demon's essence. It was somehow stronger, more powerful.

"How did it manage to get stronger in captivity while I got weaker?"

Dave Forest was puzzled. For the first time, he knew fear. His heart began to beat rapidly as thoughts continued to race through his head. "I may have underestimated this devil. I will need a champion to assist me."

He began to calm himself and regain his composure. He looked around again, making sure his actions didn't bring attention to him. With a slight gesture yes to himself he walked to their family car.

When they arrived at his family's house, he quickly retreated to his room in an effort to discover more about the person whose body he had chosen to occupy. The angel, P'an Ku, quickly found a mirror and looked himself over, seemingly not amused by the mortal body he now controlled.

That evening at dinner, the family sat and watched as Dave sat there staring at them; not saying a word, not touching his meal, simply studying the men, women, and children that surrounded him. The family simply shrugged off his behavior, figuring he'd be okay in a couple of days. After dinner, they all retired into the den. An uncomfortable silence lingered in the room as the possessed man sat motionless, still studying his new environment. His nephew, Bobby, picked up a small ball and shook it vigorously, sounding a bell inside which attracted the attention of the family dog.

"Mom! I'm going outside to play with Jonjon," Bobby called out.

"Okay, but be careful and stay out of the street," replied his mother distractedly. Soon afterwards everyone heard the sound of screeching tires and a sickening thud. Rushing outside to see what had happened, they saw Jonjon lying in the street. He had been struck by a speeding car. The small dog lay at an impossible angle, whimpering on the side of the road.

P'an Ku ran over to the boy who was stunned in horror as Jonjon tried to drag his crushed body to some non-existent haven. Bobby's mother and father rushed out to comfort their son. P'an Ku rushed to the animal, kneeled beside it and whispered gently into its ear. Carefully, he slid his hands underneath Jonjon. With great reverence, he lifted the dog and walked back into the house. "Let me get him inside and make him comfortable," the elderly angel said. "Better keep Bobby outside."

Once inside, P'an Ku rushed up to his host's room and laid Jonjon on the bed. He closed and locked the door. A warm shimmer could be seen seeping through the cracks of the door, and within moments, a loud crunch and an ear-piercing yelp reverberated through the house.

In a panic, Bobby flew through the doors, rushed upstairs and crashed against the locked door.

"Jonjon. Oh my God, Jonjon!!!" cried the young boy. "What are you doing to my dog?"

He was quickly joined by his father who, unable to restrain himself any longer, pounded on the closed door.

"Dave! For heaven's sake leave the dog alone. There isn't a darn thing anyone of us can do now! Open this door now!

At that moment an eerie silence fell over the house. Slowly the door opened and out slid Dave. Unexplainably, his appearance had changed. His hair was no longer a solid raven black, but now had several thin, silver-white streaks through it. Even more pronounced was the fact that his eyes had apparently changed from their dark brown to a peaceful, swirling hazel. Behind him lay the motionless body of Jonjon.

Bobby cautiously approached the side of the bed holding Jonjon's toy ball. As he looked upon the body of his lifeless pet, he began to cry. Reaching to hug the dog, the ball slipped from his fingers and struck the floor sounding the bell within it. Suddenly the dog's body shuddered.

"Jonjon?" he asked in shock.

At the sound of his master's voice, Jonjon turned his head and reached for him. To everyone's amazement, especially Bobby's, Jonjon jumped up into the boy's arms, licking his face like there was no tomorrow.

"My God Dave. How is this miracle possible?" asked Dave's father.

P'an Ku said nothing. In the den, he sat smiling as he watched his host's family come one by one down the stairs. Each had a look of disbelief as to what they had just seen. Dave's father looked at his son with great concern. "How did you do that? What happened to your eyes and your hair? My God, it has silver streaks in it. Look Dave.

"If this is some kind of a joke we are not amused," squawked his mother. He raised his hand and replied, "It's been a long night. I'm going to bed." The house grows silent as Dave (P'an Ku) left the room.

TWELVE

WHACK! THUD! SPLAT! The sounds of cracking shells echoed through the night as a hail of eggs exploded against the door of old man Weatherspoon's house. Leo and Tony had been planning this for about a month. "That'll teach that old coot not to take things that don't belong to him," shouted Tony.

"Well, if you could catch, he would never have taken our ball," retorted Leo.

"Yeah, well if you knew how to throw right, I would have caught it," Tony rebuffed.

Just then the porch light came on.

"C'mon, let's go. He's coming out!" Tony whispered.

Leo slipped on the grass moistened by the night mist. As he tried to regain his footing, the front door sprang open. Old man Weatherspoon stepped outside just as the boys escaped from view. Laughing hysterically Leo spouted, "Man is that old coot gonna be pissed. Do you think he saw us?"

As both boys moved quickly down the street, Leo noticed that Tony had fallen behind. "Tony? Hey Tony? Let's go! What the hell are you doing?" asked Leo.

"Dude, shut up!" replied Tony, pointing at the roof of the Forest family home. "Look!"

To their surprise stood a naked man perched on the spine of the Forest house. He walked to the center of the roof where he sat down and crossed his legs. The man raised his hands to the sky and began to chant a hypnotic verse. The boys could hardly believe their eyes. Entranced by the chanting, they found themselves overwhelmed by curiosity. One by one the animals of the nearby woods appeared and seemed to slowly circle the house around him. Predators and prey summoned for this special purpose walked together, side by side. As a gentle breeze picked up a diaphanous vortex of clouds formed in the air, engulfing P'an Ku. His hands reached to the heavens, straining as if reaching for something familiar. Over the horizon, three swirling rainbows danced in the heavy darkness of the night sky. As the colors approached through the fields, their movements tightened as they were consumed into each other. As the dancing lights came to a full stop over P'an Ku, his body stiffened as brilliant energy swirled out of his body. Instantly the vortex closed and appeared to be yanked back into the heavens.

Snapping out of their stupor, Leo turned to Tony. "What the HELL! What the HELL! What the HELL was that!"

"I don't know, Leo. Let's just get out of here."

Tony started to run home. Halfway down the street Leo looked back to catch another glimpse of the naked man. As he looked back, he tripped over his own feet, his momentum carrying him into a couple of metal trashcans. As the trashcans fell clattering to the pavement, Leo looked up, realizing that he was in the driveway of his own house. "You idiot!" yelled Tony.

Just then the bedroom light in Leo's parent's room flickered on and the window blinds shot up, revealing a frightened older man. The man's fright turned to anger as he recognized the clumsy intruder.

"Goddamnit boy!" he shouted. "What the hell do you think you're doing. Margaret! Your damn son, I repeat, YOUR son is groveling outside in the trash with his useless friend, Tony. Both of you boys get your asses in this house. I'm calling your dad, Tony. Does he know you're out at this hour?"

"But dad there was..." SLAP!

"Shut up, boy. Get in your room!"

✳   ✳   ✳

Early the next morning, a heavy whack of the newspaper careening off the porch woke the naked P'an Ku. He looked around to find he was still on the roof, cold and wet from the night air and morning dew. Realizing he was naked; he broke a branch from a nearby tree to cover himself as he sneaked back into the house to dress. After dressing, he headed downstairs for breakfast. As he crossed the den, he noticed on a coffee table near his feet lay the local newspaper with the headline reading "Local Hero Saves Mother and Child from Would-be Carjackers." It was followed with a picture of Joe Jeager. Picking up the paper he read on and smiled. He now knew the face of the one he sought, the one who would bring hope.

THIRTEEN

P'AN KU ARRIVED at the address that was given in the newspaper story he read and found the school closed with a note attached to the glass door which read:

Classes canceled due to family emergency
Will open next week.
Thanks for your understanding,
Sensei Joe Jeager.

P'an Ku placed his left hand at face level on the door, lowered his head and closed his eyes. He sensed the despair and sorrow but he knew where to find Joe.

Friends and family had gathered at the cemetery to pay respects to Joe's grandmother. Joe was surprised to hear that today was supposed to be the worst day of the rainy season. The weatherman had predicted a ninety-five percent chance of rain with gray skies approaching. As he looked around, the birds filled the skies and squirrels scurried by on the resting grounds. He could feel the warmth of the sun's maternal rays as he looked up to see the silky white clouds.

He thought to himself, "This is not a day for a funeral."

To everyone's amazement, tiny swallows would dart from the surrounding trees and momentarily flutter over the flower-covered casket, as if bidding farewell to a good friend. Joe squeezed Michelle's hand tightly and turned to her, putting his lips close to her ear. "She always attracted all sorts of wildlife," he whispered.

Off in the distance by a tree, P'an Ku stood waiting for the opportunity to introduce himself to his soon to be successor. As the funeral came to a close Joe turned to Michelle and pulled her tight to him. "When we get back to the funeral home, I'll drive you home."

"Are you going to stay with me?" Michelle asked, a little worried about her fiancé.

"No," Joe replied. "I need some time to work out, you know, clear my head. If you need me, I'll be at the school."

Michelle simply nodded as she wiped the drying tears from her eyes.

An hour later Joe pulled into his usual space in front of the school. As he exited his car, he heard arguing and scuffling, as if someone was being pushed around in the alley next to the school. He decided to investigate the commotion. As he entered the alley, he discovered two thuggish-looking men pushing and thumbing through a stranger's pockets. It appeared that the stranger needed some help. He recognized the two men as being local troublemakers who had before harassed some of his students. He found this the perfect opportunity for pay back and to release some of his soul-numbing anger.

They pushed the man to the ground after finding nothing of value on him. The two men turned to walk away, but Joe stepped out in front of them, cutting off their escape. "Did you boys get what you needed?" He asked, rolling up his sleeves.

Before any words could be spoken Joe sprang into action. Balancing himself on one leg, he spun around on his heel, lifting the other leg into a cocked position. The thug's eyes widened just as Joe completed his spinning thrust kick connecting with the thug's sternum. The force of the attack sent him flying into the other, smashing their heads together with a wet thud.

Looking down at the groveling pair on the pavement, P'an Ku began to snicker. "That will teach you to mess with an old man." He looked up at Joe and smiled. "Thank you, my friend. I knew you would come."

Joe smiled back and looked at the two worthless jerks lying on the ground.

"Guess it's about time someone took out the trash!"

He reached down and picked up the smaller of the two, dragging him to a nearby trashcan. He deposited him head first into the receptacle.

As he turned his attention to the other, he was surprised to see the stranger holding the larger of the thugs above a trash can with one arm, and then releasing him into the receptacle below. Joe wasn't quite sure he had seen what he thought he had just seen. Something just didn't sit right with him.

"Come with me, I'm going to call the police. Are you okay?" he asked.

"I'm fine," replied the stranger.

His eyes took in the lavish facilities. P'an Ku asked, "What kind of training facility is this?"

As the two entered his office, Joe looked back at the strange man. "Guess you have never been in a dojo."

P'an Ku looked around the office, impressed by the beautiful antique oriental paintings. He spotted a glass cabinet that contained several antique swords and small statues. He made his way toward the cabinets to get a closer look. "I see you are a collector."

"Something like that" Joe replied.

There on the top shelf to the right, close to the glass, stood a faded, worn down, hand carved panda. P'an Ku placed his hands on the glass as he looked down. Waves of memories long forgotten fell upon him as if they had happened yesterday. A tear filled his eye as the panda brought back memories of the sweet little boy who had died at the hands of Satan's sentinel. The flashes continued of the young boy who was always happy and smiling, so full of energy. Never once was the boy without his panda.

P'an Ku jolted as a flash of the boy being dropped onto the streets of the village, throat slit, filling him with feelings of intense anger. The vision of the boy's mother crying, falling to the ground and arms flailing, filled his mind's eye with the anguish and sorrow she felt long ago over the death of her son. The purpose of him being there was made even clearer as yet another flash entered his mind. This one, of the boy's uncle clenching young Chen's wooden panda on the battle field, he is intent on revenge. All this took place in a split second.

"Hey, are you all right?" Joe asked. "Do you need medical attention?"

The old angel was brought back to reality by Joe's voice. "Yes, I'm okay. I'm wasting too much time. I have to tell you something that may seem far-fetched to you, but you must believe me for what I am about to tell you will alter your life forever. To make a very long story short, my name is P'an Ku, and I have taken over this body. I am a spirit from a long, lost time ago. I lived in the Huang He valley in the year 2516 B.C. I was engaged in battle with a very savage and brutal demon. By some unknown force, we were captured and imprisoned to this day. I was released a short time ago, only to find that my adversary had been set free sometime before me. He is very, very strong now and is getting stronger as we speak. I need your help."

"Help for what?" laughed Joe. "You want me to help you exercise a demon? You got me all wrong, pal. I'm a teacher, not a priest."

"That is exactly why you were chosen, you are a fighter, but not just any fighter." P'an Ku eyes were fixed on Joe. "I have chosen you for the purity of your heart."

"What the....?" Joe responded. "What are you talking about? You don't know anything about me."

"When you saved that lady at the supermarket, you didn't have to help, yet you didn't turn and walk away. You remember the promise you made to yourself when you were younger, that when you became good enough in the martial arts you would help all those who could not help themselves."

"Okay. Okay. This is a joke, right? What... have you been talking to some of my students?" Joe sneered.

P'an Ku's eyes were still fixed on Joe. "Did you really think that I needed your help in the alley? It was just a ploy to meet you. I knew you would come to help me because I knew your heart is good. But purity of heart is not enough for what lies ahead. I must train you for the most challenging, most deadly fight of your life. You must know this now! The souls of all beings alive now and for generations to come rest in your hands." "The purpose for your birth has now come to pass."

"With all due respect, sir, you're freaken loony!" Joe mocked. "I think you better leave!"

Disregarding Joe's command, P'an Ku walked to the center of the training room and began to stretch out. "Listen here, child, you are in no position to demand anything after that pitiful display in the alley!"

Joe's eyes grew wide as the anger built inside. "What did you just say?"

"Your skills, boy. They are lacking and we haven't much time," P'an Ku replied.

"Okay, you stupid son of a bitch. I didn't want to have to do this but I guess I'm going to have to. No one, and I mean NO ONE comes into my school and insults me or my style."

As they squared off, Joe was irritated by the stranger's indifference. From about 10 feet away, Joe, in a controlled charge, released a series of powerful lunge punches aimed at P'an Ku's chest. As he moved in, it was as if he was staring into a strobe light. P'an Ku moved to his left about an inch before literally disappearing.

"Oww, !!" Joe yelled as P'an Ku reappeared behind him giving his ear a viscous flick with his finger.

"I told you; you are a child to me." P'an Ku chuckled.

"Okay, okay, time to take out all the medicine because… the doctor is in… the house," Joe retorted with a cocky tone.

He began to bob up and down and dance around the mat. This time he dove into a roll, flipping his legs upward, trying to strike his opponent in the chest.

Once Again, he felt the familiar smack to his ear. "Damn it!"

Now enraged, he sprinted full force toward his opponent, jumping into the air with a flying thrust kick. Stepping forward at a 45-degree angle, P'an Ku released a barrage of blows. The first blow made contact with Joe's groin, doubling him over in midair. The rest striking various pressure points. Before reaching the mat, his upper body was stinging from the multiple strikes that had lashed his upper body. Frustrated by the fact that he could not do anything to this stranger, he stood up and lifted his shirt to reveal many welts that resembled hand prints on his chest and stomach.

"Bah! You're all right. Those were just love taps." P'an Ku replied.

Joe looked in the direction from which the voice came from. There, leaning up against the far wall was P'an Ku. He held in his hand a wallet, keys and several dollar bills evenly fanned out. From the wallet hung several pictures.

"Is this your woman?" asked P'an Ku. "She is very beautiful. I bet she knows that your heart is good."

"What the hell? What are you doing with my wallet?" Joe asked as he prodded his pockets to find that their contents had been removed. "Give me my stuff back. Uh, how did you do that?" Joe asked.

P'an Ku snickered as he returned Joe's belongings. "Like I said. Your skills need to be worked on... By the way there are a couple of dollars missing. I need them for the bus."

As he left the school, P'an Ku half turned to his new student. "Your training begins tomorrow. Be ready."

"Yeah, yeah! Whatever," Joe replied.

FOURTEEN

MICHELLE ENTERED HER house she discovered flickering candlelight's with the aroma of roses, coupled with the scent of French vanilla that filled the entryway leading up the stairs. She smiled as she saw a trail of rose buds scattered in a path leading up the stairs as well as candles that lined the stair well with Joe's clothing thrown randomly along the way. Michelle saw a shoe, and up a few steps on the stairwell a sock, Joe's shirt at the door of her bedroom and his pants by the foot of her bed.

Michelle stood in the doorway of her bathroom to find Joe in her large oval bathtub filled with bubbles surrounded by candlelight and a fresh bouquet of flowers with wine poured just waiting for her to enjoy.

"All this for me! You must be feeling better." Michelle asked.

"Well, my other girlfriend couldn't make it so I guess you'll do." Joe stated.

"Oh really?! I bet she doesn't have a body like this." Michelle replied.

Joe watched Michelle as she entered the bathroom and gave her a look that she knew what he wanted. Joe watched the silhouette of Michelle undressing slowly for Joe's pleasure as she entered the tub.

Joe embraced Michelle with a sensual embrace as they kissed. Joe had a chocolate covered strawberry that he began to hand feed Michelle, and held a glass of wine for her to sip with the wine dripping down her naked body Joe licked the wine off her neck, Michelle began to laugh since she was so ticklish and they both slid into the tub.

The light from the full moon overhead peeked through the bedroom window as Joe reached for scented oil from the bed. He poured a little on his hand and smelled the fragrance and gently rubbed Michelle, massaging her body with the oil.

Joe tells Michelle "I love you Michelle, I could never love anyone more than I love you, right now."

"I love you too my sweet." Michelle said.

"Promise you'll never leave me," Joe asked. "I need you".

Michelle whispered, "I promise".

Joe and Michelle embraced and kissed passionately.

Later that evening, Joe was sitting up against a large wooden headboard with Michelle resting her head on his shoulder, running her fingers over his chest. The soft sheets entwine both of their hips.

Michelle looked up at Joe who was staring out the window and asked. "A twenty for your thoughts?" Joe looked at Michelle and smiled. "Whatever happened to a penny for your thoughts?"

Michelle smiled back. "Inflation, Honey".

Michelle's stare turned to concern as she sat up. "Do you want to talk about it?"

Joe replied with a pain filled voice as tears filled his eyes. "I miss her so much."

"When I went to see her, she looked great. I don't know what happened she became hysterical when I gave her a hug." Joe shows her the dark purple bruises left on his upper arm caused by his grandmother during her convolutions. "Look at this"

Michelle grimaces. "Oh, that looks like it hurts."

"No, it doesn't. But at the time, I didn't think too much about it. For once I didn't know what to do, or say… I was really scared." Joe admitted.

Michelle gently responded, "It's okay to feel that way, honey, there was nothing you could have done. It was time for her to go. I truly believe that everything happens for a reason."

Joe growls. "I'm so mad at her for leaving me! I know that sounds selfish but I wanted her to see us married and see her grandson, if we ever have one." Joe smiled at Michelle, hugged her tenderly.

"Yes, I wanted that too. But don't you mean granddaughter." Michelle teased.

"Do you want to know something else? I can't get this name out of my head. I heard it very clearly after her seizure ended. She looked at me and tried to tell me something, but her words were all jumbled up. She kept repeating the name Celesthargor." replied Joe as he turned and looked into Michelle's eyes.

"Would you know what that means?"

Michelle gave Joe a puzzled look. "No, but I'll try to find out what it does tomorrow, okay?"

Michelle picked up a pen and wrote the name Celesthargor on a note pad near the phone and stuck it in her briefcase.

Loud slaps and yells reverberated off the walls of the dojo as P'an Ku entered the school. Joe looked to the entryway to find P'an Ku standing there with his hands on his hips. Joe motioned to one of his black belts to take over the class. He approached P'an Ku. "What the hell are you doing here?"

"It is tomorrow. Tomorrow is now today. It's time to begin your training," responded P'an Ku.

"But I have a class to teach," said Joe.

P'an Ku walked over to Joe and put his arm around him, whispering in his ear. "These are your students, and you have trained them well. However, what is it going to do to their self-confidence when they watch their master get his butt handed to him by a flabby, middle-aged man? They don't know what I am. All they see is this shell that I have possessed. So, I can either train you now or embarrass you in front of your students or we can start privately. It is your choice."

"Wait, wait. Let's go into my office," Joe stated, flashing back to the beating he received the previous night.

As they entered the office, P'an Ku turned his attention to the panda once again. Without hesitation he seized Joe's hand, applying pressure to several points, causing great pain. Joe submitted and followed him to the cabinet. The angel opened the cabinet, removed the wooden panda from inside the cabinet and placed it in Joe's hand. He then wrapped his own hands around it. Immediately, Joe began to spasm as he was launched into the past.

FIFTEEN

2516 BC HUANG HE VALLEY, CHINA (YELLOW RIVER VALLEY)

THE BLADE WAS cold and extremely sharp. Chen didn't dare breath. His mother had warned him about straying too far from the village. As usual, he had ignored her warnings. Now he would pay for it. He clutched a wooden panda in his fist. It was his only remembrance of a father who had died when Chen was just three springs of age. He recognized three of the warriors from a settlement a couple of miles south of his. He assumed the fourth man was from their village as well. As he felt the knife pressed to his throat, Chen's senses were sharpened almost to the point of pain. He could hear the massive trees around him, their limbs swaying slowly in the air. The pungent smell of rotting flora assailed his nostrils. The air was heavy and, dank and wet as the mid-afternoon sun spilled in through the dense canopy of the treetops. He heard cries from many creatures sheltered in the rain forest and briefly wondered if they could smell his fear. He closed his eyes and, in pain, resigned himself to his fate. His body stopped trembling as the terror was replaced by the bitter calmness he found in his acceptance of death. As he felt the men lift him and move over the hills to their village, the fear of the unknown overwhelmed the young child, causing his resolve to dissipate. He began to cry for his mother. The next few minutes felt like hours as Chen was half dragged; half carried across the rugged terrain.

A man was waiting for them as they entered a clearing at the edge of a village. He was crouched before a small fire, his scarred face almost hidden from view by shadows. He looked up at the men carrying Chen and smiled almost imperceptibly. Chills' enveloped Chen's body as his eyes caught glimpse of his devilish captor. The man's face gave no sign of emotion. Rather it was the brightening of his cat-like, bloodshot eyes that gave away his demonic intentions.

Chen closed his eyes tight as the four men held him by his limbs, two men pinning his arms behind his back with the other two binding his legs together. Chen opened his eyes once again in time to see the man before the fire nod at his captors. He held his breath in an effort to keep from screaming. His people believed it was an unforgivable sin to scream like a woman in childbirth, to die without honor. He felt his head pulled back as far as the muscles could strain. A knife pricked at his throat before slashing mercilessly through the soft flesh. Chen lost all control, and screaming until the blood filled his lungs and his world went dark and silent forever.

The man before the fire picked up a small bowl and walked to where Chen was being held. He lifted the bowl and caught the crimson liquid as it gushed from Chen's lifeless body. The man reached out as if to close the boy's eyes but did not. He nodded at the four men who silently moved in shuffling steps a small distance away and dropped Chen's body into the moss and mud of the forest floor. Disposal would be dealt with later. They returned to their master and stood before him.

The man held the boy's life force before him in the bowl, the flames from the fire licking at the vile container. He lifted the vessel slowly above his head and began a quiet chanting. The henchmen stood as apparent prisoners of the soul. As the evil figure stared at the sky, an eerie darkness descended on the clearing and the village beyond. He lowered the bowl slowly to his lips and drank the warmed blood. Rivulets of red ran past his disfigured cheek sizzling as they dropped into the fire. The bowl dropped into the flames, and the man stared closely as the fire hissed, flared and danced as it enveloped the clay dish. He looked in the direction of the village and then began to shake slowly. He glanced at his quivering forearms which were swelling and pulsating with his heartbeat. The shaking became more violent, and then he stood. Tenaciously, he strode towards a large tree at the fringe of the clearing. He stood before the tree for a moment and looked toward the darkened sky. With a look of entreaty upon his face, he slowly lowered his arms staring at their pulsing strength. His left arm dropped loosely to his side. His right arm slammed into the tree trunk, shattering fist-sized chunks from the wood. He cracked blows on the trunk until the land was covered with shattered bark and pulp. He paused for a moment, reminding himself to save his strength for the events to come. Without warning, a stream of blood surged from his nose. He turned away from his disciples so they would not see this apparent mortal weakness. He wiped his nose clean with his forearm. Very slowly he turned to the men and signaled them to follow. With long, purposeful strides he entered the small hamlet and made his way to a modest rise in the center of town. He called out to his followers to surround him and listen.

"I am to be the Great Provider! I and I alone can make the fields green and the crops grow! I can heal the sick or punish the wicked! I bring you this!"

He pulled a metal knife from his tunic and held it up before the crowd. A shaft of sunlight broke through the gloom and gleamed on the metal. The villagers stepped back in surprise. "Have no fear my children," the Great Provider replied. "This will help you in war and peace. I will show you how to use this to gain power over others in the land. But before we can enjoy the peace that power brings, we must destroy the Evil One. His disciples are controlling a nearby village. We must all go there and destroy them. If you fail, the Evil One will enslave you and your families. He will have every male castrated so that he and he alone can fill your wives and daughters with his seed."

The people murmured to each other. They had never suspected evil lurked this close to their home. But if this warrior, this Great Provider, told them that it was true, they must believe him. They must do just as he said to preserve their way of life. The men in the crowd began to talk among themselves and grew angry at the thought of the evil that was so near to them.

"Good. Let the hate burn inside you!" the Great Provider retorted. "I will teach you to use weapons and fight like great warriors. Within one moon's turn, we will attack and defeat this evil."

He looked around the circle of upturned faces and noticed more than a few skeptical expressions. "For those of you who do not believe, I send you a sign."

The air became heavy and thick with humidity. Static electricity filled the air. The hairs on the villagers' bodies began to rise. A heavy pressure fell on their chests. They looked at each other. To their surprise the clothing on their bodies was clinging and folding onto itself. From overhead and without warning **BOOM!... BOOM!... BOOM!!!** Within the guts of the dark, murky clouds that covered the land, crackles of lightning pounded out with such anger! It forced the people to their knees, arms flailing over their heads in sheer terror. Suddenly the clouds parted and stars began to peer down from the heavens, spiraling and darting across the night sky. The villagers whispered to each other as the sky appeared to be filled with golden rice. None of them doubted the power of the Great Provider any longer.

CHAPTER
SIXTEEN

THE WARLOCK FOREST

THE FLAME FLICKERED as he walked towards the table. He glanced around the room at the dozens of candles burning. Their dancing flames calmed him and helped him to focus on the task at hand. He bent to open a large scroll on the worn teakwood table in the corner of the room. His silken robe brushed against the edge of the scroll. Feeling the warmth from the candles, he reached up to adjust the robe on his shoulder. He un-wrapped a piece of leopard skin, the sign of wisdom, from his body and placed it next to the scroll. He picked up a crude feather pen and began to make the exacting symbols of his language to spell out the incantation he knows is forthcoming.

After he finished writing the recipe of the spell he was about to use, he laid down the scroll and turned to a smaller stone-topped table in the center of the room. He removed two unfinished crystals from a worm leather pouch and laid them down carefully in the center of the table. There was a noise behind him and he turned to see an old woman bearing a bowl of rice and beans and a cup of water. He then turned back to the shimmering crystals.

She looked at the man with concern. "Fu Hsi. Even the greatest wizard has to keep his strength up by eating!"

She tapped her foot as he turned and looked at her with feigned exasperation.

"Alright, alright old woman," Replied the old man. "You are worse than the squawking birds in our woods."

He sat on the step in the doorway and looked at the meager meal as she pushed the bowl at him. "Eat!" she replied as she creaked herself down beside him.

"Why do you work so hard? You haven't slept for days now."

"You know why," he growled. "Since I was six springs in age, I've had a vision of what is happening in our land right now. I have prepared my entire life for this moment. All that practice and all those mistakes have finally paid off."

As a child, he had been given the vision of an evil prophecy. Two powerful warriors, a champion from heaven and a demon from hell, would come forth to the mortal realm to face off in battle for control of the living. The two warriors would lead mortal armies in the battle to end all battles. Both sides would be so evenly matched that this war would never be won by either side and would bring destruction to the living world, killing all of man in the process.

One man will be given the power to contain both warriors. As the first battle of the war begins, he must rise above the battlefield, recite the holy incantation, and entrap the two powers forever in eternal darkness. The angel will forever keep watch over the demon, preventing him from returning to earth and clearing the path for Satan's rule.

After the vision, he was given a recipe for the holy spell. To this day, the vision is as clear as the first time it entered his dreams.

He gulped the meal down quickly and began to laugh, the sparkle returning to his tired eyes. "Oh, and God knows I've made many mistakes."

The old woman laughed for a moment at a memory. "Do you remember when I had bad corns on my feet? And you tried to fix that problem?"

The old man chuckled in embarrassment. "Yes, yes I do."

"And you made it worse by turning my foot into a large chicken's clion." They both dissolved into laughter at the thought of simpler times.

"Sorry, but I corrected that problem didn't I. By the way, that happened... what... hundred and fifty springs ago?"

"One hundred and eighty-five to be exact." The old women replied.

The old man smiled again, but then his face clouded with worry. "I don't know if I can do this. I don't believe I have the strength left for it."

"You are stronger than you think!"

The old woman patted his knee and smiled encouragingly at him. "Remember, I have watched your magic grow stronger and stronger through each passing winter."

She turned towards him and grasped both his hands in hers. "Besides, I believe in you. You can do this. God have chosen you for this task. He works through you, Fu Hsi. You will not be out there alone."

"You're right. Thank you for giving me the strength to continue."

He put his arms around her and hugged her warmly. "You know something? For every good wizard there is also a great woman at his side."

He patted her hands as he held them, smiled at her, then stood up. "Enough. It is time for me to work."

The old woman gathered up the bowl and cup and left the room with a smile on her old wrinkled face. Fu Hsi walked back to the stone table in the center of the room. Drawn on the floor were special runes with blocks of lines that pointed vertically and horizontally encircling the table. Each block represented the different aspects of the universe, Heaven, wind, mountains, earth, thunder, fire, and water, according to his beliefs. His magic was composed of these elements. The wizard gathered his strength and lifted his hands up over his head. Sparks flew from his long, golden nails. A circle of energy traveled up his frail body and around the delicate bones of his hand. He made a brilliant ball of energy, which seemed to change colors in the candlelight. Then, with a blast of air from his mouth, Fu Hsi floated the ball of energy like a bubble to the center of the runes. He began a chant low in his throat and almost unheard. When the iridescent sphere reached the center of the stone table it popped. The air filled with a golden dust that seemed to circle the room. The wizard continued his chant, growing louder with each passing moment.

Outside, a dark cloud developed in the sky and settled itself high above the straw roof of the little house. A bolt of lightning streaked down and entered the dwelling, striking the stone table. The room briefly filled with a thick haze. The man of magic began to cough as the smoke filled his lungs. When the smoke cleared, he could see the two crystals he had set on the stone table had turned into beautiful decanters. One of the decanters was a melon-sized crystal with a dark purple center. On the outside was a secret form of calligraphy traveling vertically on the crust of the crystal container, warning outsiders to beware. The other was exactly like the first but the center was a beautiful turquoise blue. On both sides of each decanter were four brilliantly crafted, elaborate dragonheads, guardians used to ward off any who should find the relics. These would be the eternal prisons for the supernatural warriors.

CHAPTER

SEVENTEEN

THE WOMEN WERE screaming frantically. Yok Fong ran out of her hut to see what the commotion was about. She saw four men coming down the dirt path through the center of the village. They were carrying something wrapped in animal skins. The men were strange looking—cold, almost inhuman in their matching dark clothing. They stopped in the center of the village and dropped their bundle. The women crowded around keeping their children safely behind them. Yok Fong looked for Chen but didn't see him among the children. The men began to unwrap their bundle. One of them was standing just in front of Yok Fong, obstructing her view. She looked at his hands and stared for a moment at the dragon symbol burned into his skin. The design went all the way from his hand to his elbow. The dragon circled his wrist and shot fire up his muscular forearm. She glanced over his shoulder and saw her mother, Lin Yun scream and fall to the ground. The man with the dragon on his arm moved away. Yok Fong saw why her mother had screamed. There in the dust lay her son of only ten springs of age, Chen. His throat was slit from ear to ear. It was obvious he had been drained of his blood. It stained his face and body. Yok Fong shrieked as she ran toward the men. When they grabbed at her she noticed that they all had dried blood on their hands. She did not let them slow her as she raced toward her child's body. She swept him up in her arms and wailed at the sky. All around her, people were yelling, trying to stop the men that had returned Chen.

Just then, P'an Ku, the village healer and wise man came into the crowd. He was a bit of an oddity. He towered above the other villagers with almost an 'otherworldly' quality. His smooth complexion and long hair were snow white, his eyes piercing blue. His chiseled features gave him an overwhelming sense of authority. This was a man to be reckoned with. However, looking into his eyes one could not help but see that he was a gentle and compassionate man. Though he wore a long, white robe and sandals, the dirt and dust of the village streets never clung to him or his garments.

"Stop! Stop!" Everyone calmed down. "What is the meaning of this?"

P'an Ku turned toward Yok Fong. She could see a tear form in his eye. He stood before the four men and held out his hands. "I asked you, what is the meaning of this? I want an explanation. Now!"

The men stepped back a little but regained their composure quickly. "This is a warning from the Great Provider. He knows the evil you are working here and he will make it stop! One moon cycle from today he will meet you on the field of battle to prove his power. You have until then to prepare."

The four men turned and began to walk out of the village. The people began to rush after them but P'an Ku held up his hands to stop them.

"Stop, my friends. They do not know what they are doing. Did you see the dragon's head and the flames of orange and yellow covering their forearms? They are controlled by a very powerful demon. They are Long Fa, the dragon's fire. They are what burns. They are sent to do the work of the dragon. I was afraid this day would come."

He turned to Yok Fong and held out his arms. She walked slowly toward him, tears streaming down her face, her son still in her arms.

"I am so sorry for your loss, Yok Fong. Chen was a wonderful child and will be missed by all. His death was not in vain. It is very sad for you, I know. But he has gone on to the next life and is happier there. I will see that he has a proper burial. When our time of mourning is done, we shall prepare to protect our families and village."

As he took young Chen from Yok Fong's arms he paused to embrace her for a moment. As he brushed her skin, in her mind's eye she was momentarily sent to another place, a large pasture surrounded by lush green trees opened before her. There her son stood smiling and happy. In an almost involuntary reflex, she draped her arms around him and kissed his face. Smiling and laughing, he hugged her back. He then pulled away and made his way toward the far end of the field. Chen began to run as if being called by some unknown utter. A sudden feeling of love and peace came over Yok Fong. Then, the soft, warm voice of P'an Ku pulled her back to the here and now. "Oh, thank you! Thank you!" she replied gratefully, the tears still streaming down her face.

With a knowing smile, P'an Ku nodded. As he walked slowly away from her, she sank to the mud of the street, her heart breaking. She lay face down in the dirt and felt her mother's arms around her. She looked up at her mother and took the small wooden panda from her hands.

After the burial ceremony, P'an Ku called all the men of the village together. "We are facing the greatest challenge of our lives. It has been said that The Dragon will send his best to make way for the dark ruler to conquer our world. This beast is very powerful and can take control of the souls of those who are unaware of his power. It is this demon that has taken control of those men and the village to the south of us. He now controls our brothers and sisters like puppets. I have lived among you as one of you for many Springs, waiting for the day the dark one would show itself. I have been sent to lead you against the dark one. Together we can confront and defeat Dragon's minions. We soon must face off against this great evil. I know that some of you have friends and relatives in our neighboring village. They are no longer who they once were. This beast has taken their will. We must overpower them at all costs. I have brought this to help us."

He held up a small piece of metal. "This can be heated and turned into weapons of all types. I will teach you how to make weapons before I leave to prepare myself for the coming battle."

P'an Ku spoke longer to the men and over the next few weeks taught them many things before he left. He assured them that he would return to the village the night before battle.

"Mark well what I have taught you," P'an Ku preached. "Continue to practice and hone your skills, for when I return, you must be ready to face the evil that plagues us."

After many days' journey into the mountains, P'an Ku sat on a high cliff looking toward the sunset. He fasted and prayed to his God for almost seven sunrises without an answer. He would make one final plea before returning to the village. Tomorrow would be the toughest battle he had ever fought and he knew that the souls of the villagers, as well as his own, were at stake.

He mixed herbs and mystic powders into a small bowl and added to it water from the sacred spring, the source of all life on earth. He heard the animals of the forest come to him. He needed their strength now more than ever. As they passed by him, P'an Ku reached out and took a small piece of fur from each animal. And replied, "thank you tiger for your gift of cunning, thank you panther for your gift of speed, thank you wolf for your gift of courage, thank you monkey for your gift of play, thank you deer for you gift of agility and jump, thank you panda for your mystic powers and gentle strengths." He mixed the fur of all the animals—with the other contents of the bowl. He glanced up at the sun. Just a few more moments and it would drop behind the mountains to the west. He swirled the contents of the bowl once more, then stood. He glanced around at all the animals then raised his arms quickly, throwing the mixture into the air above him. Nothing happened for a moment and he feared that he had failed once again. Suddenly, there was a great turmoil of winds around him. He felt the animals come closer to him to protect him or be protected by him he was not certain. The winds swirled around him; the thunderous noise almost unbearable. Then before him came a great light. He looked toward it and saw a swirling rainbow. It came toward him from the mountains in the west and hovered above him. He reached toward it and felt himself rising through the air. He looked back and noticed his physical body fall to the ground and the animals move close, lying close to his body to provide warmth and protection. He moved quickly toward the sun, eager to meet with his God, sure that his Deity would grant him the power to vanquish the harbinger of death he and his people must confront.

C H A P T E R

EIGHTEEN

WHEN P'AN KU awoke, the field was dark. The animals still surrounded him. He felt the great sense of power and righteousness in the course of action he had chosen. He gathered his meager belongings and began the trek back to the village. The animals trailed him on his journey lending him protection and companionship.

When he entered the village, everyone came out to see him. They had been making preparations of their own and felt they were ready for the coming battle. Yok Fong was one of the first to see him. She ran from her hut to meet him but stopped midway when she saw the light from an almost full moon fall on the animals that followed him. He motioned her forward and she walked timidly toward him.

"Have no fear, my child. They will not hurt you. They have merely accompanied me on my journey." P'an Ku replied.

Yok Fong was surprised at the change in P'an Ku. He had obviously lost weight and his hair had grown a great deal. It was nearly to his waist now. But his eyes were the most stunning difference. They were no longer a deep blue but a bright, almost metallic green. He hugged her and then took her hand as he walked toward the center of the village. The villagers crowded around P'an Ku. The men had brought their new weapons tainted in poisons made by the secretions of the fluorescent frogs of the rain forest. They were dressed for battle. Half of their bodies were painted black with a red dot in the center, and half painted in white with a black dot in the center, representing the struggle between good and evil. The women crowded close to their men, anxiously waiting the moment when they would leave for the battle. The children stood in wide-eyed silence.

"Greetings my family. I hope you have been well these past days. I have returned to you now and am ready to lead you into battle. I feel we have the power of good behind us and will triumph this day."

The people applauded and cheered wildly. P'an Ku circled the crowd, laying hands on each and every warrior to give him strength and blessings. The animals stood outside the circle unafraid of the humans. Seeing that their beloved master was in the company of friends, they retreated back into the protection of the forest. When P'an Ku had finished with his rounds, he asked the men to demonstrate the skills they had honed while he was gone. P'an Ku was very impressed with their progress.

Soon it was time. The women tearfully kissed the men good-bye promising to keep the children safe and wait for them to return.

The morning dawned cold and misty. Dew hung from every tree and every blade of grass. The men of P'an Ku's village arrived at the battlefield in good spirits. They took their positions and waited.

The anxiety of war was apparent among the men. The smell of Litchi berries, coupled with the light aroma of the Wax Apple trees, permeated the air. As they waited, some of the men picked peaches from the surrounding trees. Some looked around at each other and wondered who would survive, and who wouldn't. P'an Ku scanned the field. Throughout the rolling hills the morning fog slightly draped the many small purple flowers that poked their heads out of the ankle-high grass. Everywhere he turned and looked, life was flourishing and it was hard for him to believe that this beautiful meadow would soon turn into a bloody field of death.

The Great Provider had led his men on a long and difficult march. They had been ripped from their families twenty-four sunrises before and made to practice their skills from dawn 'til dusk. They were tired, worried, and anxious about the coming battle. Many considered fleeing when they saw the great numbers of opposing warriors, but knew it to be certain death to show any sort of cowardice.

The two leaders walked to the front of their respective armies. They came within a few yards of each other before stopping. The Great Provider looked at P'an Ku with a sneer and a lift of his dark brows above piercing red eyes. P'an Ku gave him a firm glance, his green eyes dancing with light, undeterred by the devilish figure that stood before him. They took measure of each other carefully then turned to rejoin their men.

P'an Ku reached his men then turned to face the opposing army. He watched as the Great Provider walked back and forth before his men irritated by something. The warrior demon stopped near the end of the front row of soldiers before a boy of no more than sixteen springs. The Great Provider nodded and the four men with dragons on their arms emerged from the ranks and grabbed the youth. The demon grabbed the young man's hair and pulled back his head. He turned to look at P'an Ku, a horrible grin crossing his face. He turned back toward the youth struggling against his captors. He pulled a long-sharpened piece of bamboo from his pocket and stabbed the young man's neck, ripping the stick across his throat with great force. Blood began to spurt from the severed artery, spraying the men around him. They stared at the Great Provider as the boy's essence covered them. A look of pure blood lust crossed their faces. The vital liquid poured down the bamboo stick as the demon pulled it out and sucked on the end. He dropped the stick in the dirt close to his victim. The blood gushed from the wound. The Great Provider opened his mouth to receive it. When he felt he had taken enough power, he turned back to P'an Ku and his villagers, many of whom were retching quietly in the grass. He smiled wickedly at P'an Ku, blood dripping from his face and mouth. P'an Ku gazed angrily at him, refusing to show his revulsion.

The Great Provider walked to the center of the field to face his men. He raised his arms high above his head and then dropped them as he let out a bloodcurdling scream. He turned and ran full force toward P'an Ku and his warriors, his soldiers following frantically behind. P'an Ku's warriors answered with a war cry of their own and charged the opposing army.

In the center of the fighting, Tung Hai Chuan rushed forward with a sword held over his head with both arms. He faced off with the first man he came across from the opposing village. Ever since the death of his nephew, young Chen, he had vowed revenge against the evil one and his followers. Now he would have his chance. The man wearing war paint stood about ten feet from him, knees slightly bent, with one arm pointing toward Tung Hai Chuan. To Tung's surprise, the second man brought his arm from behind his back to reveal a shuang sou dau, (blade staff). Tung lunged his sword first at the man with the bladed staff. As his sword came down, the other man countered with the blade of his staff. The blade struck home at Tung's wrists and detached them neatly from his body. Like a switch, things turned from fast to slow motion from the adrenaline rush. In a powerful, circular motion the bladed staff continued its viscous arch. Tung was frozen with shock and unable to move as the bladed staff buried itself deep into the thick of his thigh. The pulsating pain from his severed nerves caused him to slump slowly to the ground, unable to defend himself any longer. He lay in the mud bleeding and helpless.

One of Tung Hai Chuan's fellow villagers rushed to his side. He attacked the man with the bladed staff. With great power he whipped a large wooden staff catching the fold of his enemy's legs. The dark soldier fell onto his back as Tung's friend impaled the fallen warrior in his neck with the staff; blood spewing from his mouth dotting P'an Ku's soldier's face as he squinted to avoid the spray to his eyes and mouth. The victor looked to his fallen comrade who was taking his last breath. They nodded to each other in silence as the fallen man faded away knowing that his family would be taken care of.

Across the battlefield two more men were fighting. One of P'an Ku's men carried a beautifully hand-crafted sword. One of the demon's slaves wheeled a long-hooked tooth blade and a large knife. The swordsman swung his weapon with all his might. His first swing missed and he aimed again. The Great Provider's soldier countered with his large knife. The swordsman parried the knife and swung once more and missed. He felt a stabbing pain in his abdomen. He glanced downward to see the hooked blade slide slowly into his flesh. His face went white as he dropped the sword. The man with the hooked tooth blade twisted it slowly, making sure he had plunged his knife deep enough. An evil smile crossed his face and brightened his bloodshot eyes. He lifted his left leg high enough to kick his victim firmly near the center of the chest. The last thing the victim saw as he fell to the ground was a bloody mass of his own entrails entangled to the knife, trailing from the wound. The killer raised the mass of guts pulled from the victim's wound and held his weapons to the sky, a war cry on his lips.

Nearby, two more men were fighting for their lives. Another of Pan Ku's men had a crude trident of which the middle tooth had been broken in an earlier encounter. The other man was one of the Great Provider's soldiers armed with a machete. As the man with the machete was forced backward, he stumbled over a bloody corpse and fell back against a large tree. The man armed with the trident saw his opportunity and pinned his opponent's neck to the tree with his weapon. The pinned man began to laugh hysterically, noticing that he had been spared by the missing tooth of the broken weapon. He stabbed out at the man with his machete. His blade connected with his opponent's chest and he was rewarded with the screams of his attacker. He then pulled the machete back and swung wildly at the hands holding the pitchfork. Fingers were severed and launched in all directions as the man dropped to his knees. He held his butchered hands toward the sky in supplication before he fell to the ground in death.

A few feet away two men were battling, slowly moving toward the tree. One of P'an Ku's men was armed with two fighting sticks while the other man from the opposing side held an executioner's ax. The stick fighter was much more agile and consistently held the advantage. He attacked high and low, keeping his opponent constantly off balance. The man with the ax became very angry and began to swing wildly with his weapon. The man with the fighting sticks spotted the man pinned to the tree and began to form a plan in his mind. He began to duck and dodge toward the tree, carefully hiding the man who was pinned to it, keeping his body between the attacker and the soon to be victim. He began to tease and taunt his attacker, infuriating him further. The ax man swung wildly as the man with the sticks suddenly ducked. Unable to stop his swing in mid-flight, the ax wielder glared in surprise and shock as his blade sliced through the pinned man's neck and deep into the tree trunk. The severed head flew through the air toward the shocked man. Without thinking, he dropped his weapon and caught the bloody orb. It slid from his hands and landed with a thud on the blood-soaked ground. Seeing his chance, the stick fighter moved in quickly and twisted his opponent's neck sharply, killing him instantly.

In the midst of the savagery of fighting, darting in and out of harm's way was one of the Great Provider's personal guards. The small brute of a man sported custom made straps containing slender darts of hollowed bamboo. Leather straps wrapped every major limb of his body providing him with easy access to his volley of darts. The darts themselves were morbid works of art. Each painted with its own unique prayer of death. The tips were lacquered with the venomous secretions of the forest frogs that inhabited the area. The darts were constructed so as to be more efficient in penetration. Each hollowed to provide space for a small, dense stone that, on impact, would strike the tapered edges of the dart, driving it further into the victim. His appearance was just as menacing as his weapons of death. His hair was pulled back and tied in a ceremonial bun; streaks of white in his hair accentuated his sharpened features. Skillfully placed in his bun for easy access were even more darts. His entire body was freshly carved with intricate patterns of death; the cuts themselves were swollen and still bleeding, giving him a maniacal look that intimidated his opponents. The night before the battle the small brute was seen with glazed over eyes huddled before a fire with numerous knifes of various shapes and sizes placed on a leather skin, arranged like surgeon tools. The brute picked up a knife and his eyes become beguiled as if being summoned by the dead.

Then, like a flash, he darted in and out between the battling warriors, not once being touched. In a simultaneous motion, one hand retrieved the deadly darts and the other anointed his victims. One by one they were paralyzed, allowing his fellow soldiers to reap the benefits of victory.

Off in the distance the dark slayer spotted the omniscient figure in white and moved toward him. P'an Ku and the Great Provider had worked their way towards each other in order to fulfill their destinies.

The ambitious dart thrower, seeking credit for the demise of his master's enemy launched a dart as hard as he could towards the unsuspecting P'an Ku. Engaged in battle, his senses were heightened to their extreme. He heard the faint whistling of the oncoming object, alerting him of the immediate danger. With great skill, he simultaneously kicked, breaking his opponent's knee sending him to the floor while plucking the dart from the air. Amazingly enough, P'an Ku caught the dart of death by its rear and immediately launches the projectile back to its owner. Surprised by the amazing speed of P'an Ku, the dart thrower was unable to react in time as the dart drove home deep into his eye, causing his head to recoil back. As his head jerked back, another of P'an Ku's soldiers, wielding a war hammer, slammed his weapon into his head, crushing the bun coated in poisoned darts deep into his skull, lodging them into his brain.

From within the center of the battlefield, on a small rise stood the Great Provider and P'an Ku. The two gave each other a level gaze, measuring the mentality of their opponent. The Great Provider's gaze wavered just slightly and P'an Ku smiled in satisfaction. The two began to circle each other, oblivious to the fighting going on all around them.

The Great Provider attacked first, lunging toward and kicking at his opponent. P'an Ku blocked the kick with expertise, turning the tables on the demon with a barrage of blows to the face and chest. The Great Provider stumbled back in shock, holding his mouth and chest. P'an Ku could see the anger growing in his eyes along with a look of wariness. Again, they began to circle. The Demon attacked again, using his fists to pummel P'an Ku. Once again P'an Ku was able to block the attack, this time by trapping both of the demon's hands and striking a death blow that kills slowly to his chest. He followed with a viscous uppercut that caught the Great Provider just below the chin, violently snapping his head back. The demon backed away staring at his chest. Slowly he looked up at P'an Ku. The imp tasted the blood in his mouth and knew his time was short. As it spilled from his lips, he spotted a nearby villager who had emerged victorious in his fight. He looked back at P'an Ku with a sneer and suddenly raced to the nearby villager. With a powerful lunge the demon wrapped his left hand underneath the villager's right arm, his right arm slapping across the victim's left shoulder blade. He then interlocked his hands in a deadly embrace. As their chests met, they were momentarily fused together creating a doorway to the new host. Widened by pain, the villager's eyes could now see the full extent of the ordeal taking place. There before him stood the Great Provider. With disbelieving eyes, the man he knew as a god began to show his mortal frailty. Under great internal stress, the human figure began to writhe in pain. His face slowly bloated as the pressure increased within his body. As the demon took what it needed from its old host, capillaries began to ooze causing the skin to take on a dark plum color. Cherry red pellets of crimson liquid beaded on the tightened skin of his brow and cheeks. In a sudden burst, a river of blood flowed from his nostrils, streaming down his face and coating both men's chests. The Great Provider began to convulse, his body shriveled. Each limb became sunken and dried slowly curling into the direction of the trunk. The body, dry and frail, unable to sustain the weight of its limbs, fell to the ground with an inanimate thump. Sneering at the spectacle before him, P'an Ku watched in disgust as several sharp talons flaring with electricity pulled the skin of its new host shut for its concealment. Again, the pair faced off.

Just then, from the distance a powerful chanting was heard engulfing the theatre of war. The villagers stopped and cautiously backed from each other, keeping a weary eye on their opponents, and scanning the area. On a high cliff overlooking the field stood the great wizard Fu Hsi clad in garments of tan and forest green. Hanging from his sash were several small pouches containing the fur, feathers, and skins of various animals from the Warlock Forest. They were anointed in mystical oils to emulate their strengths and attributes. Standing with his hands raised to the sky, his chanting became more pronounced. His hands began to glow. He reached into an old leather satchel resting on the side of his hip. He quickly flipped it open and retracted the decanters, spilling out the luminescent glitter of silk tracers. He once again raised his hands up to the sky, this time hoisting the decanters. His eyes, in a trance, were fixed on the heavens above. Two large black clouds began to form over the wizard's head, slowly traveling to the center of the combat zone. They came to a rest directly over the two battling spirits. Lightning filled the sky as the clouds began to move in a circular motion. From the opening, small objects began to fill the air. Billions of tiny winged beings, sparkling in the darkness, spiraled down amongst the villagers, freezing them in their tracks.

P'an Ku and the Demon gazed around at the scene. They looked up at the wizard as the two crystal containers began to glow. The containers opened with a blue beam of light swirling from them. The light turned and was directed toward the two spirits on the battlefield. They were frightened and pained by the light. It seemed to act as a vacuum pulling the souls of the spirits toward the containers. Brilliant light of all colors danced overhead as the two entities fought against the wizard's power. Each was surrounded by a thick beam of light. They started to shake but froze in place like the mortals around them on the battleground as the light engulfed them. The light became brighter and brighter until their souls were being wrenched from their bodies. The two spirits struggled as they were pulled toward the light. As they fought to stay within their bodies, hands and arms appeared from the light, pulling at the mortal frames causing the two warriors to lose their grasp on their mortal hosts, and rising into the sky.

The souls swirled for a moment in the light. Then with a great popping noise, they disappeared into the two crystal containers; P'an Ku into the turquoise, the Demon into the purple and black. The wizard emerged from his trance. He put the containers into separate animal skin pouches and glanced up as the clouds scattered above.

Sunshine began to pour down on the villagers. They stared at each other in wonder as the tiny winged beings vanished. It seemed their clothing had changed during the mêlée. Instead of dark clothing on one side and light on the other, the villagers all wore varying shades of gray and green. It was difficult to tell the two sides apart. Feeling the new found freedom from their demon captor, the ragged warriors dropped their weapons and began to help each other. The wizard smiled down at the villagers. "The Demon and the Cherub have been imprisoned from this realm!" shouted the wizard. "Their battle will no longer be ours! Return peace to the lands and see to your families and each other! Evil shall haunt us no more!"

He then slowly turned and walked away, never to be seen nor heard from again. Throughout time folklore and legends were told at campfires and at mealtime of the tragic events that befell the land. Village storytellers sung songs of this great wise man. Whispered stories and legends were all that remained of the man that saved our world.

NINETEEN

JOE PULLED AWAY from P'an Ku, his body trembling from the images that rushed into his mind. "What the hell was that, Old Man?" asked Joe, wiping the sweat from his brow. I was there, I know what has happened.

"I'm sorry for the abrupt way that was presented to you, but we have little time and you had to learn what you are up against, why you are here. The Demon we seek killed that boy and many others in the weeks that followed. He is here to open a path for Satan's rule on earth. If he is not stopped, all of mankind is destined to fall victim to the pure evil that will come with Satan's rise."

"But that is a demon, and I am just a man. What good will I be against it?"

"That, my dear boy, is what the training is for. From your heart's purity, I will teach you to pull forth a power that you have never known. A power that the demon will not be able to withstand. But we must start now. Are you ready?"

"Yes, yes, it is time." Joe stammered as he rushed out and cleared the class. "Class is over, and the school is closed until further notice." Joe replied to his students.

Answering several quick questions, he assured his students that classes would begin as soon as possible. Joe locked the door as the last student walked out and training like he had never been put through began.

Joe was pummeled and then was shown the ancient fighting technique. He repeated the technique several times, forced by pain to remember.

Dave barked and mocked Joe. "Relax! Relax! You're too rigid! Stop using so much strength! You are so slow I can time you with a calendar." Dave spouted.

Dave continued to pummel Joe who was becoming very frustrated and battered. Joe muttered under his breath. I can't do this shit! What does he mean too much strength?

Dave stopped the training. "Joe, stop! Listen. Let me ask you this question. Which is stronger—the trunk of a 200-year-old Oak tree or a single blade of grass.

Joe looked up at Dave with a puzzled look. "Anyone with half a brain knows the Oak tree is a hell of a lot stronger than a blade of grass, come on now." Joe replied.

"Typical answer, and at first glance that would seem so, but when a hurricane comes, the branches of the Oak tree are torn off and the trunk is snapped in two and pulled from its roots. However, the blade of grass just lies back until after the storm has passed, then it comes right back up." Dave stated.

Joe paused for a moment. "I think I understand but still don't think I can do this. You're having me do things I've never seen before. Are you sure this is gunna work?" Joe questioned.

"Believe me, pain is the greatest teacher. Remember, be like the blade of grass, and let the power flow within you."

Joe began to absorb everything he was taught like a sponge. With each day to come he was pushed to new limits as he was still pummeled.

His skills developed seemingly beyond his own senses. The intensity of his training made him wonder what it is he will be up against.

One morning Dave the old angel showed Joe two tennis balls attached to two six-foot ropes. Dave proceeded to swing the ropes above his head and below his ankles, changing directions simultaneously at first Dave started out slow then continued faster than the human eye could see.

"What on earth is that?" Joe said.

Dave replied. "Ahh, I see I've captured your interest."

"Well, are you going to tell me what it is" Joe replied. "Or do I have to guess."

"Be patient my boy. All I will tell you is this will quicken your skills."

"Show me WHAT!" Joe questioned. "How in the hell am supposed to do that if I can't even see it." I don't expect you to learn how; just don't get smacked you can do this by feeling the air brake around you."

"Ok," Joe replied. "I feel the air, now what do I do?"

Dave had begun to smile a mischievous grin as he approached Joe swinging the ropes. "Good," "now don't get hit." Dave retorted.

After Two weeks of training, grinning at each other Joe and Dave squared up with a look of I'm going to kick your butt, both held butterfly swords ready to attack. Joe struck Dave first with the swords raking against each other with sparks flying in all directions. Dave quickly cut the watch off Joe's wrist not touching his skin but simultaneously Joe swung his sword to Dave's neck with the dull side of the blade resting on his throat. Dave smiled at Joe.

"Good," Dave responded. "You're almost ready. But first I must show you the final test. If you survive you pass, and then you will be ready."

"O crap" spouted Joe. Wondering what crazy thing Dave was going to come up with next. Joe walked into the warehouse to discover six ten-foot-tall large metal inhuman devises in a moon shape arrangement, the devises were metal tubing and had many arms, three of which had knife's protruding outward with the other three metal stumps dangling. Behind the devises were steps leading to a walkway. On the rails were various weapons hanging like marionettes with Dave at the control.

Joe thought to himself it must be inhuman, this thing I must fight as he questions Dave.

"When did you have time to make this?" Joe replied.

"I slept for over four thousand years." Dave replied. "I don't need sleep."

"Ya right!" "So, what do we do now?" Joe asked.

"WE don't do anything," but YOU will need to fight this creature and win." Joe looked at Dave with bewilderment.

Dave proceeded to explain the rules of engagement for what Joe must do to win.

Joe moved into the attack position in the center of the devices waiting for Dave's instructions.

"I want you to touch one of the metal arms before we begin". Dave commanded. As Joe touched the metal arm he was met with a blue ark of electricity, sending a shock through his body. Joe's body was jolted back as he grabbed his hand that was just shocked. "Damn!" Joe yelled, "What are you trying to do, kill me!" "No," said Dave, "but it will. Now lock up with the metal monster."

Joe locked up in a fight position pointing his swords towards the front of the metal giant.

"Ok, you have one minute to reach the top of the platform" Dave instructed, "and striking the head of the monster will shut off the electricity. There will be areas that have no electricity, you must find them but they will only last for a few seconds. Good luck. Tell me when you're ready." Joe took several heavy deep gasps of air.

"Ok, I'm ready." Joe said.

Dave flipped a switch as two buckets of cold water fell on Joe drenching him. "What the...." Joe yelled.

Dave interrupted. "Ok, go!"

Joe used the appendages as steps to climb from one to another swinging and slashing his swords. He launched an attack at anything that came at him, Dave was adding to the challenge by swinging the marionette weapons at Joe. Joe yelled when small bolts of electricity shot through his body. The electricity was shut off, as Dave was surprised, due to the fact it had only been twelve seconds.

"I knew you could do it," Dave said. "Amazing what a little pain does for your speed."

"Why am I training against such awkward attacks?" asked Joe hurt and angry, "No human can attack like this."

"That's right." Dave replied. "I'm not training you to fight a human, but something far greater than you can imagine. I just hope I have trained you well enough to defeat it."

"Yeah, well what if I decide not to fight it when it shows up." Joe mocked.

"My son," Dave said. "Oh, you will fight it. Not only will you fight it, you will seek it out. It will have taken everything that you love and destroyed it. You will do everything in your power to kill it, even if that means the giving of your own life. Remember, we all have a time to die. Every one of us will meet death it is unavoidable. Just pray yours isn't any time soon."

Joe and Dave left the warehouse as Joe's hair began to rise off his head from the electricity. Joe tried to pat his hair down and rubbing his sore butt.

"I couldn't find one spot that didn't have electricity in it." Joe said.

"You're right, there wasn't any." replied Dave with a smile.

TWENTY

THE SOUND OF sizzling bacon could be heard throughout the house. Christine, Jesse's mother, was crying softly while making breakfast for the family. She heard a young voice behind her. "Mom I'm hungry. What's for breakfast?"

In shock, she dropped the spoon and spun around. Her heart skipped a beat as she saw her little boy back to normal. She dropped to her knees and hugged Jesse tightly, sobbing. She already decided that Jesse would be going to the hospital by ambulance early in the morning but now Jesse appeared well enough to be taken to the hospital in the family car for an examination to try and find out what had happened. Several hours went by before the examination was completed. The doctor came out and invited them into his office. He sat them down and explained the results of the testing. The doctor told both parents that Jesse was completely normal and very healthy. There was nothing to worry about. As for what they had witnessed, there was no current medical explanation. He suggested taking Jesse home and to just keep an eye out for a relapse.

Later at home, Jesse told his mom he was going up to his room to play on his computer. "Okay, honey, I'll have lunch for you in about an hour," Christine replied, happy to see her little man back to his old self, unaware of his real intentions.

A few minutes later Jesse climbed out of his window and down the trellis. As he walked along the sidewalk, he came to a small, metal fence about two to three feet tall. As Jesse ran his fingers along the fence he came to a break. He stepped in and walked through to the schoolyard. Halfway through the schoolyard, he was confronted by the six bullies that had terrorized him throughout the school year. "Hey, there's Jesse, and it looks like he wants to play," laughed one of the bullies.

"And we know just the game, don't we, fellas," laughed another.

With a calm look and clear eyes, Jesse looked to see how many kids were around. He smiled with an evil glare and quickly blinked his eyes. The upstroke of the blink revealed eyes that had become blood red with a feline look to them. One of the boys spotted the change in his eyes and stepped back. The others followed. The leader of the group, the one who had held Jesse up against the lockers took the first bold swing at Jesse's face. Jesse smiled and swiftly turned his body and tapped the oncoming fist off target, sending it plummeting into the face of one of the other bullies. Laughing hysterically, Jesse sensed an attack from behind by another. This time he felt the cold, sharp instrument sliding past his skin deep into his kidney. "Oh shit!" Jesse responded as he quickly reached back, grabbing a hold of the handle of the instrument that pierced his body. He paused just long enough to make eye contact with the boy who had stabbed him. Smiling, he slid it out and electrical currents darted out, dancing across the blade as it was pulled from his wound.

Taking the now bloody knife in hand, he faced the attacker. The young boy backed away as Jesse skillfully slung the sharpened object at the little punk. The boy fell to the grass, shaking in pain. He plummeted into shock and then blacked out. One of the boys on Jesse's right side swung a chain, trying to hit him in the face. Jesse took the brunt of the hit to the face without moving an inch. He reached out with his right hand and grabbed a hold of the chain. The other remaining boys saw his large, bony hands with long, broken fingernails. A look of astonishment ran across their faces. With lightning speed, Jesse took the chain and quickly wrapped it around the young man's wrist, throwing the boy into the other gang members. The others pulled out their weapons, homemade sticks and knives. Jesse used the young man's body as a weapon. He wielded him around with such great strength. Nothing could be heard over the torturous pain-filled screams. To everyone's surprise, the boy was launched, leaving behind the skin embedded into the now bloody links of the chain. Jesse then dropped the chain and looked at the other boys as they began to yell and scurry around him, trying to find an escape route. Jesse then lifted both arms in front of them and made two fists. Six-inch daggers of bone shot out through his knuckles. As each one attacked Jesse, he hit a vital spot of their body with his daggered knuckles. After a few seconds the fight was over. Jesse looked around to find six carcasses badly mutilated. As the daggers retracted back into his hands, he turned and walked away. With an evil smile he blinked as his eyes returned to normal. Without a backward glance Jesse walked away aimlessly, as if nothing had happened.

Jesse found himself on the seedier side of town. Hookers and drug dealers were hanging out on the dirty sidewalk. Across the street he saw a triple X theater and adult video shop in full swing. He knew he was in the right place. Jesse passed an entrance to an alley where he spotted three men that looked like bikers and a bleach blonde hooker. One of the men had the woman up against a wall, her pants at her knees and bent over. The biker had his pants to his ankles and his hands on her hips, straddling her "Yes!!! Yes!!! Yes!!! That's its big boy!" she screamed. I see your mama taught you well baby!

He grabbed a handful of her hair. "Yes!!! Yes!!!" At that moment the hooker looked over and spotted Jesse.

"Hey! Hey! What the hell do you think you're looking at?" she yelled.

Jesse just stood there with a smirk on his young, innocent looking face. The biker was startled and stumbled slightly, backing up and pulling up his pants.

"You better get the hell out of here you little pervert!!

The other two bikers laughed at their pant less friend. "Animal, you better watch out. He looks pretty tough to us!!!"

Animal, a medium built black man, turned to Jesse. "You think he looks tough?" he growled to his friends. "I'll show you tough!!! You little shit!"

He zipped up his pants and rushed toward Jesse. The apparent little boy was calmly standing there in the middle of the alley with an amused expression on his face as he blew a bubble with a piece of gum he'd been chewing on. Animal assaulted him just as he expected, lunging at Jesse with a punch to his face. Jesse blinked and the ever so recognizable eyes of the demon of blood appeared. Animal tried to pull back but it was too late. Jesse redirected the attack with his right hand. Using the back portion of his hand and folding it at the wrist, giving the appearance of a praying mantis, he moved his hand straight up to Animal, attacking first at the tender portion of his forearm. The arm went flying back, allowing Jesse's bony fingers to shoot toward Animal's shoulder and sink them, passing through the epidermis, grabbing a firm hold on the muscle and wrenching it out just enough so as to leave it still attached to the bone. The skin pinched the muscle at the base creating a mushroom shape. Animal stood there paralyzed in pain and before he could even get off a scream, Jesse kicked his left knee out from under him, breaking the joint completely apart. Animal fell to his right knee and was now the level of the little boy. With great agility and speed Jesse maneuvered behind Animal taking his right hand and placed it under his chin placing his left hand on the right side of the man's face at the temple. He buried his two middle fingers deep into the biker's pain-filled eyes. Swiftly pulling up and to the side with a snapping crunch, Animal dropped with a heavy thud to the pavement below.

The blond-haired hooker ran off in horror, stumbling in her high-heeled shoes. Weasel, who was leaning against a wall stood up in shock. "Holy shit. What the hell did you just do?"

He looked at Animal's battered body. "You son of a bitch. I'm gunna kill you!"

Weasel approached Jesse with slight apprehension. Jesse stood with one hand out in front of him. "Don't hurt me. I didn't mean to do that. Please! Please don't. I'm sorry."

Weasel was now feeding off the fear of the begging young boy who was backing away from him. He reached for his arm, but to Weasel's surprise the young boy grabbed his forearm and twisted, pulling up on the arm, causing the bone to splinter and puncture through the skin. Weasel's face looked to the sky as his teeth ground tightly together from the pain. Jesse raised his right fist, level with his victim's eye. Tiny drops of blood flecked from his knuckles as three dagger-like bones ejected themselves from under the skin, coming to a stop about twelve inches long. The demon boy shot an uppercut at the man's crotch, the blades coming to a stop at the small of his back. Weasel erupted into violent convulsions and dropped to the ground; another soul headed on the slow, painful trip to hell. Jesse quickly faced off with Spider who was so terrified he could not move from the spot where he stood. Jesse's young little body started to vibrate and change in shape; his clothing ripped and fell from a body that could no longer sustain them. Popping, cracking and tearing sounds were coming from inside Jesse's transforming frame. In one quick burst his chest blew open, the sounds of the chest cavity flaring, throwing the soft internal organs against the hood of Spider's car, and creating an exit for Satan's soul collector. The beast began to emerge from Jesse's abdomen. First a foot that had only three toes with eight-inch spiked hoofs. Another foot followed as the body exploded!!!! The ten-foot beast awoke from within its old host and stretched out onto the street as the pavement buckled underneath its gargantuan weight. It moved quickly and awkwardly toward its new host. The Beast faced Spider. From one of its gigantic arms, a bone scimitar flashed from its wrist. The demon roared into the night, bringing the blade down slashing into the man's tattooed chest so fast that there was no pain. The creature grabbed its stunned victim, pulling him close. Electricity filled the air as the demon forced itself into the open cavity. Thousands of miniature lightning bolts streaked from one end of the gash to the other, pulling the wound closed like stitches done by a surgeon. Moments later a pitiful scream was heard echoing off the nearby buildings.

Spider stumbled out of the alley knocking over trashcans in the process. He appeared intoxicated as he stood at the edge of the sidewalk trying to flag a cab, awareness fleeting from him as the parasite fought for control. A bewildered look passed over his face as he felt a strange sensation between his legs. He looked down to see that he had urinated in his pants. He then looked up and chuckled, the last laugh he would ever remember.

A few moments later, a cab stopped and let Spider in. The driver was a full-bearded Arabic wearing a maroon turban. The demon, now in full control of his new host, fell into the back seat and requested to go to a bar called The Grand Grimoire, a name he found in his host's head. A fitting place he thought, Grimoire meaning the gathering of evil spirits for celebration. The cab driver looked in his rear-view mirror and replied.

"Are you all right?"

"Yeah! Yeah! Let's go!" retorted Spider.

On the way to the bar the demon looked at his mortal arms, amused by the constant wave of ripples moving to his hands. The sensations were painful but also pleasurable, like an itch needing to be scratched. Soon they arrived at The Grand Grimoire.

The cab driver looked back at Spider. "Are you sure you are, okay?"

Spider ignored the question. "Are we there?" he groaned. "Hey, man, let me out behind the bar. I think I'm going to be sick and I don't want anyone watching me, all right man!" Spider asked.

"Okay. Okay," the driver said. The popping sounds of gravel coming from underneath the cab grew louder as they reached the back. The cab driver looked into his rear-view mirror in time to see the reflection of his death. Spider's eyes had changed into the large, fiery red eyes of Celesthargor, the slayer. His mouth stretched back and hundreds of fangs seemed to push out through cold, blue lips. The cab driver froze in horror. Spider, with unimagined intensity, grabbed the driver by the chin hair, wrenching him up and back over his seat. As his back cracked in half, the demon buried its snout into the twisted broken neck, causing the man's right leg to vibrate violently.

✳   ✳   ✳

The door of the cab opened and Spider stepped out, his hands coated with blood and bits of flesh. He reached back and tore a strip of clothing from his victim to clean himself. As his face contorted back to normal, he mocked, "Who said sand-niggers tasted bad." The door slammed closed and he staggered toward the bar.

Sitting at a table in the back of the establishment, Spider entertained himself by emitting strings of electrical energy through his beer, causing it to boil over. Just then the front door exploded open and a group from the local fraternity spilled into the bar. He looked up in irritation and decided to move toward them in hopes of a confrontation. Staggering from side to side he purposefully elbowed the drinks out of their hands. One of the men at the end of the group shoved him away. "Hey, you asshole, what the hell do you think you're doing?"

Spider turned toward the loudmouth and whipped his right arm up, pointing at the unsuspecting punk. Large ripples of skin and muscle ascended from his elbow to his wrist. The back of his hand shattered with a violent release of internal pressure, spraying the crowd with crimson fluid. A shard of bone pierced through his wrist, looking like a knife had appeared in his hand. With blinding speed, he rammed the instrument into the man's eyes, exploding out of the back of his head. He pulled the bone from the man's head, the body slumping to the ground. The crowd reeled away from him in shock. Spider then turned to face his next fool-hearted victim. At the end of the room stood a large man in a western blazer, white shirt, jeans and boots. As they made eye contact the man reached into his coat pocket to reveal a snub-nose 44 revolver. He pumped two rounds into the chest cavity of Spider, leaving two gaping wounds. Still standing he backed off slightly from the impact of the bullets. He then looked at his wounds and begun to violently spasm. To everyone's shock, a large thin object, still encased by skin, flared out from the breastplate. As the skin reached its elastic threshold, the point of the object cut through, causing it to snap back and issuing forth deep, red life fluid across the faces of several on-lookers.

Revealing a sword that became razor sharp with every passing moment screams and gasps could be heard. Loud ripping and tearing echoed off the walls of the now silent bar. Blood and bile covered guts splashed on a nearby crowded table. At the same time a second and third blade appeared, one located on his back, and another hammering upward through the chest and trachea. It caught Spider's body just behind the chin cutting through his face, the blade sticking out about twelve inches past the center of his forehead, causing the body to split in half. The beast began its birth, revealing its true self. A thick, muscular leg with three large talons pushed through the abdominal cavity onto the blood-soaked floor. At the same time another ripped through the lower back, bracing itself in preparation of birth like a disfigured fowl fighting through an egg. The remaining carcass fell to the floor as the beast began to realign its joints. His joints popped and cracked as he stretched and flexed every muscle and tendon, realigning his body for the awakening. The blades of death would rapidly contract in and out, guided by thick tendons in an orchestrated performance on the mammoth forearms of the creature. When Hell's general completed its change, it stood a good ten foot tall. Its two sets of huge pectoral muscles danced rhythmically shaking the pasty entrails off its body. Shifting now from side to side it scanned the layout of the surrounding vicinity. Without warning, it gave out a shriek so intense, so bone chilling, everyone in the establishment froze in utter terror. One of the local frat boys soiled his pants before running for the door. The beast spotted the bar owner which happened to be the one that shot at it. Their eyes met again. The bar owner known as Rene to all the locals froze. "Holy shit! What are you?"

He lowered the gun and dropped it to the floor, knowing that bullets would not stop the monstrosity that had emerged before him. With an animalistic ferocity the demon bolted toward the terrified man, clearing a path, splintering tables and chairs, causing debris to fill the air in the surrounding area, rushing to embrace its new host.

TWENTY-ONE

MICHELLE ARRIVED AT the lab where she works to find her assistant, Bobby Lee, sitting at a lab table looking into a high-powered microscope. She always found Bobby amusing due to the fact that he would change his appearance daily. She snickered as she saw that now Bobby sported a sleeveless lab coat bearing a multitude of strange tattoos on his skinny arms. Underneath he wore a purple tie die shirt and filthy, torn, pulled out of the trash jeans. His heavy oriental features clashed with his bathroom bleached blond hair. She hastily tossed her cell phone, purse and briefcase onto the table and turned to a chart, unaware that the contents of her briefcase had spilled out.

Bobby, with his heavy California beach surfer dialect spouted, "Whoa, Barbie babe. Did your Ken stand you up, or are you just happy that I paged you?"

She looked at the chart. "Has the blood test from the lab for the Jane Doe murder come back yet?"

"If it was a snake, it would have bitten you. They're right in front of you." Bobby stated as he turned curiously to the fallen contents of the briefcase.

"Celesthargor?" He laughed as he picked up the piece of paper. I haven't heard that name in years."

Michelle turned and asked, "What? You've heard of that name? What does it mean?"

Bobby looked at her with a sly grin knowing that he finally had something to barter with. "What's it worth to you, Babe? Lunch? Nah! Dinner maybe? You're not married just yet. How 'bout one last fling." He winked suggestively.

She could not hold her anxiety any longer. "Okay. Okay. I'll buy you dinner, you little shit. What does it mean?"

"Okay then. When I was a lot younger, I dabbled into the occult and Prince Celesthargor is supposed to be the right-hand demon to the most-evil emperor dude." He shook his head.

"Hmmmmm. How can I explain this in terms that you will understand?" He paused. "Ahhhhh! Have you ever watched a war movie?" Michelle nodded.

"You know how they always have someone to be the point man. One who would go way ahead of the platoon and scout for snipers, ambushes, and booby traps, clearing a path and making it safe for the rest of the men." "Yes" she replied.

"Well, he is the one sent to clear the path here on earth for the arrival of Beelzebub, the supreme chief, the demon big dog, and his soldiers of Hell."

Michelle stared at him with a blank look on her face. Bobby continued. "Michelle this is real. This is very real and pray to God that he never comes to this realm we call earth. He is the nastiest of all demons, dude. Lucifer, Astaroth, Yama. In whatever language or religion, the ultimate evil or Emperor of Darkness has existed."

He looked at Michelle with a devious smile. "You know something else... I have a tattoo of what he is supposed to look like. Wanna see it? Now don't get all hot and bothered, Barbie babe. Wouldn't want your man beatin my ass cause I stole his chick."

He removed his lab coat and took off his shirt to reveal a slender, well-defined body. There on his back right shoulder blade was a horrific picture of a beast on an elaborate throne. In his right hand he held a huge scepter which hosted a flame, representing the eternal hell. At his feet the words, "Satan: Enemy of Life". To his right was a step that came to a cliff with many jagged points. There stood a four-armed, four-legged foul beast engaged in battle. It was covered in blood from the angels it had slain. Beneath its feet, a mound of fallen angels supported his heavy frame, entrapped by its massive arms. An angel appeared to scream in agony as its wings were ripped from their roots before it was tossed aside to be later consumed. Angels flew about screaming in torment at the sight of the fallen angel. Beneath the corpses in old English, the name, Celesthargor: Prince of Death, Grand Cross of The Order of the Fly. It was followed by a strange symbol. Underneath him a series of other lesser demons stood with their names and symbols beneath them: Moloch, Pluto, Leonard, etc. In glazed fascination she emerged herself in the wickedness of the tattoo. The phone rang. Michelle jumped, bumping her head on a nearby cabinet.

"Damnit!" she winced as she rubbed her head. She grabbed the phone. "Lab 24, this is Doctor Michelle Walker."

No longer the center of attention, Bobby puts his shirt back on and sat down. Michelle hung up and turned to Bobby. "Let's go. We have another homicide." Bobby Lee smiled. "If there is one thing I love about this job, its security. There is always someone killin someone."

Red and blue lights from a host of police vehicles cascaded across the walls of nearby buildings. Michelle broke through the crowd and flashed her identification to the officer controlling the onlookers and media, signaling Bobby Lee to follow behind. As the officer lifted the yellow "crime scene" tape he stated, "We have been expecting you. Officer McCray needs to speak with you."

As Officer McCray approached with a uniformed officer at his side, Michelle smiled. "Art! It's you."

Art looked up at Michelle and awkwardly smiled. He replied with a sympathetic look on his face. "I wish we were meeting on better terms."

Michelle replied, "What do you mean?" He handed her the library card with a picture of a young male.

"This is Jesse's. What are you doing with it?" she asked.

"Look. I know you have to examine the victim's body but I am trying to prepare you for the scene. It's not pretty. The victim that we retrieved the library card from is unidentifiable. We found this in his pocket along with his wallet."

She took the blood-stained wallet from his hand. "This is Jesse's also!"

Her heart raced and her palms began to sweat. In a trembling voice she asked, "Where is the body? I have to see it for myself."

He escorted her into the alley. She saw several bright florescent tarps laying over each of the bodies. She noticed the one furthest away did not appear to be a body but just a large mass. Officer McCray led her to the one she had been staring at. He stopped just over the carcass, reached down grasping the corner of the tarp and peeled it back to reveal a large mass of flesh partially clothed. She reached into her pocket and removed a hand-held tape recorder and begins to speak into it.

"The victim appears to have no cranial region. Large clumps of internal organs scattered in a perimeter of two to three feet."

She placed sterile rubber gloves on her hands. She then lifted what appeared to be a rib cage revealing a hand with the knuckles exposed, showing a ring on the index finger. The ring contained an odd stone that she recognized. She had gotten the same kind of ring from a shaman in Brazil. He had told her it would ward off evil. Her heart went numb as she realized it was the exact ring that she had given her nephew, Jesse. The color drained from her body, and as she stood up her knees buckled. She staggered to a nearby wall where she began to gag violently. McCray turned his head to give her a moment of privacy. As she regained her composure and cleaned herself off, she cried, "Oh my God, why Jesse? Has his family been notified?"

"They are being notified as we speak. I'm sorry, I tried to prepare you."

She looked around at the other bodies and asked, "Are there any witnesses?"

"Only a hooker," replied McCray. "And she said that the boy started the fight. She also stated that the boy was very strong. She's been taken downtown for questioning and a drug test because her description doesn't make any sense."

She walked over to the bodies of the other victims and asked if they have been identified.

"This one here is Michael Bartholemeau, street name Animal. The other is Martin Hines, street name Weasel." McCray began to chuckle to himself. "I see he didn't weasel his way out of this one."

She called Bobby Lee over to take blood and tissue samples to complete her examination. Just then Officer McCray was approached by one of the uniformed officers who whispered something into his ear.

"We have a couple more for you with the same M.O.," said McCray. It's at the Grand Grimoire!"

"Can you handle this, Bobby?" she asked.

"I'll take it, get outta here," spouted Bobby.

She gathered her equipment and buckled herself into the squad car with Officer McCray. They left the scene.

TWENTY-TWO

BODY PARTS EXPLODED every which way as blood splattered the fenders and hood of the freshly painted white convertible Cadillac. Trophies of bone and chunks of flesh embedded in the grill shimmered in the light of the street lamps above. The engine roared as an elderly woman with a walking cane cautiously crossed the street to meet her nephew. She was struck down in the middle of the street by the two-and-a-half-ton piece of machinery traveling at ninety miles an hour. Her body was dragged underneath by the tires mangled beyond recognition. Her head bounced between the bottom of the vehicle and the pavement. A familiar country song blared from the Bose music system in the car. A possessed Rene grinned a sigh of satisfaction.

A few more blocks down the road he spotted a public transit bus. Noting a line of individuals waiting to board the bus, his face contorted slightly, displaying his malicious intent. He steadily accelerated and swerved onto the curb, taking aim and screaming with excitement to the horror of his victims. Their bodies shattered in two and their insides smeared over the hood of the car. Bone fragments were sprayed into the crowd and over himself. A flying bone fragment lodged deep into his face, dripping blood from his cheek onto his upper lip. His tongue darted aggressively licking his lip clean. His eyes widened with anticipation as he spotted a cyclist further down the road. He sped up and pulled to the right of the driver. The cyclist caught a glimpse of the vehicle approaching his side. He curiously looked and to his shock he saw the most horrific thing he had ever seen. A dented white fender with chunks of hair and flesh caked in blood. He then turned his attention to the driver. There in a nonchalant fashion the Demon stared forward through his host's eyes as he mechanically turned to make eye contact. As their gazes met, the demon's puppet's eyeballs spun, revealing the bloodthirsty feline pupils of the imp. Stunned by the disgusting sight of gaping wounds, flicking tongue and feral eyes, the cyclist jolted away in a terror-stricken panic, unaware of the consequences of his actions. As he struck the median separating oncoming traffic, his cycle was crushed and he was launched head first into the grill of an oncoming semi. The force of the impact was so intense that all his bones were crushed. The cyclist was reduced to a gelatinous mass, held together by his riding leathers. As the semi hit its brakes, the truck's momentum threw the carcass forward, bouncing it off a nearby station wagon. The windshield spider-webbed and the car screeched to a halt on the shoulder of the street as panicked passengers tried desperately to figure out what had just hit the windshield. The body continued on, sailing over the side of the bridge, resting grotesquely in a nearby ditch.

✳   ✳   ✳

Officer McCray and Michelle pulled up to the Grand Grimoire. They were greeted by another detective on the scene who escorted them inside. Once inside, both McCray and Michelle were almost overcome by the smell of rancid blood and other body fluids mixed with the particularly pungent smell of sulfur. She reached into her pocket and removed a small container of masking ointment and smeared a line beneath each nostril. She offered some to McCray. Without hesitation he accepted.

Both were stunned by the devastation and carnage that surrounded them. From the condition of the tables and chairs Michelle thought that someone set off a concussion grenade or some other kind of explosive device. She immediately descended to examine the remains of a badly mutilated corpse that lay nearby. McCray looked to the detective on scene. "Were there any witnesses?"

"Shit man, everybody saw what happened and many had to be hospitalized from shock," replied the detective. "None of their accounts made any sense. They say it all started with a scuffle between some drunks and the next thing you know they say that something came out of this guy. Some kind of beast." He pointed to the mass on the floor.

Michelle yelled at McCray. "Come look at this. Is this who you were looking for?" she asked as she peeled back the tarp to reveal a distorted head and neck with an elaborate tattoo of an exotic spider.

"Yup, that's our man. Guess he's no longer a suspect," McCray replied with a sarcastic chuckle.

Upon further investigation, Michelle noticed several indentations on the floor of the bar that appeared to be non-human in nature. Each footprint was coated with a light, sticky film that resembled a membrane of some type. She turned to McCray. "Could you please get me my measuring tape? It's in the box next to your feet."

Curiously, she began to measure the length of the imprint that was an exact 25 inches. She then turned and measured the width; approximately 20 inches. "My god, this thing must have been gargantuan. Judging from the area of its feet, it must have weighed anywhere from 1,500 to 2,000 pounds."

"Maybe we should talk to the bartender," stated McCray. "She says she saw the whole scene unfold."

An older woman in her fifties; blond hair, bad perm, wearing a tank top, jeans and sporting a couple of tattoos, sat in the back of an ambulance. As both Michelle and Officer McCray approached her, they noticed that she was rocking back and forth, rambling on about the end of the world. Over and over she repeated, "It's here. The end is near. The beast has arrived..."

Michelle approached the lady. As she got near, the old woman reached for her, grabbing the lapels of Michelle's lab jacket. She pulled Michelle close to her face, her eyes glazed over "I never believed them," she muttered. "But they were right. There is no way you can stop this thing. It's here and it's real..."

Two paramedics jumped into the back of the ambulance and grabbed the woman, breaking her hold on Michelle and pinning her to the gurney. The woman began to convulse, the paramedics check her vital signs, and then one of the men injected her with a sedative. Within seconds the woman was out and the men buckled her hands and feet into restraints and transported her to the hospital.

As Michelle gathered herself from the abrupt attack, another patrolman approached Officer McCray. "Uh, sir. I think you should have a look at this."

The officer led them to the back of the Grand Grimoire. Behind the building was a yellow cab, doors open. A uniformed officer was crouched down taking photos of the crime scene.

"This is a brutal one," replied the young cadet.

As Officer McCray approached the scene, his mouth dropped open in morbid fascination. There, hanging from the rear-view mirror like a pair of dice was the cab driver's head and spinal column suspended by a holy rosary. The cross of the rosary was placed, inverted, into the mouth of the head, giving it the appearance of the man being caught in mid-scream. The rest of the body lay mutilated in the back seat. For all practical purposes it had been hollowed of its internal organs.

Upon further examination of the vehicle, McCray discovered that the rest of the organs had been flung to the side of the car. The intestines had been squeezed of their contents and used to wrap a bow on the antenna like it was a gift.

On the hood of the car were strange markings, one of which Officer McCray recognized as some type of pentagram. As he leaned over to get a closer look at the markings the stench of human feces filled his nostrils. He reeled back in disgust. He turned to Michelle, holding his stomach. "Damnit that's disgusting. Whoever did this is really sick. They did it with this poor guy's shit!"

Michelle recognized the emblem on the vehicle as being exactly the same as the one that had appeared on her now-deceased nephew. She turned to officer McCray. "Thanks for your help but I can handle it from here." "Ok" officer McCray replied, "If you need anything I will be gathering more information in the bar." "Alright" Michelle smiled.

A beautiful sunrise was in counterpoint to the vibrations of a no longer finely tuned engine of the Cadillac that was keeping the demon awake. As its head gently bobbed back and forth, his eyes half open, Celesthargor realized that he had taken over a tumor infested host. Snatched from his dazed state, his body bolted upright. His orbs widen in pain. He involuntarily began to vomit tumors; his host's body was infested with them, followed by stringy masses of nerves and veins, onto the leather upholstery.

A traffic cop in his sharp uniform, white gloves, and whistle noticed an oncoming Cadillac at a high rate of speed as he directed traffic. Realizing that there was no possible way for the Cadillac to stop in time, he halted traffic in all directions in hopes of avoiding an accident. To the onlookers' shock, the large vehicle slammed into a nearby convenience store. The car half embedded in glass and brick, the car door sprung open and a badly bleeding man stepped out and stumbled toward the police officer in the middle of the street. His arm was wrenched backward and hanging by only skin. He and the officer made eye contact. The demon issued forth a spray of crimson liquid onto the officer's face as the blades of the beast began to cut its way out. People trapped in their cars watched in mind-numbing fear as the huge beast emerged from within the stranger.

As the monstrosity became fully erect, the pavement beneath its feet buckled and slipped several inches into the ground. The beast then leaped at the cop, pinning the officer to the pavement. It hovered over the officer for an instant as if deciding whether or not he was a suitable host. Its attention was directed to the crowd as cars began to collide with one another. The beast released its victim and ran across the hoods of several cars, causing them to crumble under its immense weight. As it jumped off a car onto the pavement, it greeted an unsuspecting couple dressed in business attire leaving a coffee shop with an ear-piercing shriek causing them to drop their coffee. The horrid scream shattered several nearby windows. Rocking like a pendulum, Celesthargor whipped its arms back, causing its chest to flare and dance. A plane flew over on its approach to a nearby airport, catching the attention of the beast. It then noticed the buildings that surrounded it and looked around to find an easy means of escape. In a flash, its two front legs reached out in front, grabbing a solid hold on the bricks of the wall as it forced its massive frame upward. Its two hind legs were raised to its side for balance. As it reached the roof of the building, it jumped to an adjacent building, replacing its two front legs with its hind legs. Still on two legs it darted out of sight, its screams echoed off in the distance.

TWENTY-THREE

A FEW DAYS later P'an Ku approached Joe Jeager holding a huge briefcase. "It is time for me to meet with my destiny. But I must do something first. Follow me."

He led him to the center of the room where he unfolded the briefcase to reveal a masseuse table. "Get up here," he commanded as he pulled out several towels. "Relax, lie down, and trust me."

As Joe relaxed, P'an Ku placed a folded towel over Joe's eyes and began to chant, raising his hands up to the ceiling. He took his hands and placed them palms down on his student. His palms began to vibrate and glow. Electrical currents danced from his hands to Joe's skin, causing the hairs on his body to stand. The angel's hands then moved down toward the feet to direct any bad energy away. The energy appeared as flames imploding and then dissipated. Joe arched up and yelled in pain as if something were being wrenched from his body. The ritual lasted for several hours, all of Joe's bad energy being exercised and replaced with the power of purity. P'an Ku would reach up to the heavens and pull the healing energy out of thin air! The lights that were flowing around them both was incredible! Afterward, Joe dared not move. His body felt soar and he was enveloped by a fatigue, a lightheadedness, he had never felt before. Even P'an Ku was exhausted. As Joe sat up at the edge of the table his eyes started to tear, his emotions were running rampant as memories of lives lost flooded his mind.

He wiped his eyes and turned to his master. "What have you done to me? Why am I weepy like this? Why do I feel such grief?"

P'an Ku placed his hand on Joe's shoulder. Emotions get stuck inside the body, the E in emotion stands for "Energy" and motion is just that movement. The bodies organs are made with different tissues, and when a person experience a traumatic experience the energy from their experience flows through the body and sometimes it gets stuck somewhere in an organ. I just unblock that organ from the emotion and release that stress in the body and the body starts to heal itself. "So, I ask you to, let the feelings that are buried deep inside of you go, the feelings that you are scared to open. The horror of when your mother was murdered in front of you when you were just a child, and the abandonment that you felt when your grandmother left you. Just let it go. Let your body heal itself. Believe me; you are going to need every ounce of strength within your soul. Now go home and rest. You will have the most peaceful sleep of your life tonight. Trust me."

They locked up the school and Joe went home.

✷　✷　✷

As Celesthargor sought cover at the edge of a twelve-story building, his insides began to growl indicating hunger. It spotted three potential meals hanging out in an alley by a dumpster sharing needles.

Immediately the scales on its head and back stood as it crouched closer to the building as if to attack. Its eyes honed in on one of the drug users. Intent on satisfying the craving within it, it raced to its meal. It jumped out in front of the three dope fiends. They looked up at the beast, thinking it was just part of a bad trip, not realizing the severity of the situation. "Man, I'm gonna kill Danny. He gave us some bad shit again, complained one of the crack heads. The demon stared at the three, a little pissed that they seemed not to be afraid. He singled out the one who spoke, angered by his lack of fear and respect. As the beast took hold of its victim it used its two free legs to press downward on his hips to hold him in place. The outer arms pulled the victim's limbs straight out, giving him the appearance of being crucified. The man screamed in pain, feeling his limbs being pulled from their sockets. One of the demons remaining arms draped around the head and slowly pulled it 'til it snapped from the rest of the victim's body, spraying tainted blood onto his stunned friends. The two remaining entrees scrambled for freedom. One of the junkies simply turned and ran toward the street the other one slipped and fell into some trash, landing in a seated position with his legs sprawled out. The beast tossed the head of the victim into the air causing it to bounce off a nearby wall landing between the junkie's legs. The man reeled back in disgust and horror as he went into shock. The demon then used its free arms to grab a hold of its meal's waist. Lifting the body up to its mouth, it dislocated its jaw in a quick, lustful manner.

Its serpentine tongue danced around the wound, ensuring that the veins were unblocked. Four spinning cartilage tubes sharpened in a syringe-like fashion probed forth, fitting exactly into its victim's jugular veins and carotid arteries. This happened so rapidly that it used the pumping of its victim's own heart to extract the body's life fluid. After extracting about a quart, the demon's body violently recoiled, launching its victim to the pavement twenty or thirty feet away. With several violent spasms it backed away. The demon's lips began to flutter in waves. It knew it had to expel the tainted plasma.

The poison, like an electric shock, jolted through its body. He was propelled backward into the air about thirty feet. It hit the asphalt hard, causing nearby buildings to shake from the small tremor. It pulled itself back up on its feet leaving a deep impression of its body in the ground. It opened its mouth to regurgitate the blood and bile that was tainted by heroin and aids. The combination gave it a flavor that its palate could not stand. Knowing that these were diseased hosts and it could not use them for food, it quickly left the area on another hunt, eager to find a pure source of food.

CHAPTER

TWENTY-FOUR

THE TAPPING OF keys could be heard from Joe's office as he diligently worked on his computer. A knock at the door broke the monotony of the tapping keys.

"Come on in," Joe invited.

James, his senior black belt bows as he enters Joe's office. "Come in! What's wrong?" asked Joe, noting the concerned look on James' face.

"Sensei. Why have you been neglecting to train us black belts? The others have been okay with me teaching but they hunger for YOU to make them into skilled fighters. We miss your teaching."

Joe's eyes left his students and he looked down. "I'm sorry. I've had a lot on my mind."

He turned to his computer, shut it off and walked out onto the mats. His students, waiting just outside the office, circled him and sat down, eagerly awaiting his instruction. Joe picked one of his fastest students to face him. "Today we are going to learn a new technique. One that cannot be used in tournaments, but for survival only."

Joe found it hard to stand in his usual karate stance so he changed it slightly. His students looked at each other a little puzzled by the change. As they watched diligently Joe squared off with his student. "Okay. Attack."

His student rushed forward unleashing a fierce ax kick. Like a flash of light, Joe disappeared and reappeared on top of his student, redirecting the attack and smacking him several times in the chest, sending him flying over the circle of students. Amazed at the tremendous speed and power of the attack, some swore that he had really disappeared and then suddenly reappeared on top of his opponent. The student lay on the floor stunned; the breath having been knocked out of him. Joe ran over to his fallen student, amazed himself how devastating his new skills were. He now realized how dangerous he had become. He had been trained to face death and win. This was not an art that could be taught by conventional methods. He knew he could no longer spar with his students until he learned to control his new found power.

"God Damnit!!!" Pete screamed as his wrench stripped a screw sending his hand slamming against the rusted manifold of the old boat engine. Pete Moss was an ex-Navy engineer. His hobby was repairing old boats. His unshaven face emphasized his weary features. In frustration, he stood up and took a swig of whiskey he had on the deck next to his toolbox. His six-foot frame and medium build always made it hard for him to maneuver in tight areas. He had been working on this project for several months and was not about to give up. Frustrated and drunk he decided to go to the fantail of the boat and relieve himself. As he began to urinate, he heard pounding vibrations in the distance. He paid it no mind until the sounds became more rhythmic and heavier. Whatever it was it was getting closer. He looked from side to side unable to distinguish where the noise was coming from. There was an eerie silence followed by a loud crash. The boat shook as the port side sunk, lifting the starboard end. He was catapulted to the deck, urine flying everywhere.

"What the HELL!!!" he screamed as the stream of urine splashed back onto him. "Who hit my damn boat? I'm gonna kill the son of a bitch!"

He stood up and walked to the front of the boat. Hugging the floor was a large black mass. Pete couldn't quite make out the features since the sun had just set and the object was concealed by evening shadows. "Get the hell off my boat, whoever you are!!" Pete demanded.

Just then, the dock lights came on, revealing the horror that crouched before him. There, poised to attack, was the beast. Two arms supported its heavy frame while the other two moved as if in mid-step, giving it the appearance of a giant lizard. No longer concealed by darkness, it erected itself, its arms whipping out exposing the blades of death unsheathed from its wrists. It began to rake each blade against another causing a shower of sparks to fly into the air.

Knowing that his worst nightmare had appeared before him and death was eminent, a look of hopelessness spread across Pete's face. The last thing Pete remembered as the demon bolted toward him was a blinding flash of light. Horrified screams echoed throughout the darkness.

"Sinners! Pimps! Whores! Drug Users! You are all sinners! And if you do not follow me NOW, you shall all burn in eternal hell!!" barked a street-side preacher standing on a wooden milk crate. His shiny shoes, slacks, suspenders and tie clashed with the walks of life that surrounded him.

A nearby hooker walked up and popped out a tit from underneath her tube top. She pulled up her skirt revealing naked flesh and rubbed her crotch. "Screw you, you dirty faggot! I know you want this!"

"Repent! Repent you little wrench. Jesus will not stand for this. He has told me to warn all of you. Judgment day is upon us!" he retorted, spit flying from his mouth. A car pulled alongside of him, stopping at a traffic light. The passenger was annoyed by the constant badgering coming from the street preacher. Out of irritation he threw an open can of beer, striking the preacher on his chest. The beer splashed up, lightly spraying him in the face. "Shut the hell up and go home. Nobody wants to hear that shit," the passenger yelled as the car drove off, everyone in the car laughing.

As his entreaties became louder and more aggressive a gentleman appeared around the corner at the end of the block sporting a black navy pea coat, collar pulled up, and a black wool cap. A hooker spotted the man. "Pete! Pete baby! I haven't seen you in a while. You look-in' for some action? You know honey my back door is always open for you."

She grabbed his arm and pulled him toward her to get a better look. She was stunned to find tears of dried blood streamed down his cheeks and caked around his nostrils. She pulled away in disgust. Hey man, what the hell have you been doin'?"

He pulled his arm back and pulled the lapels of his coat together as he began to shiver. He approached the preacher. Words of love, Jesus and forgiveness stinging his ears as he squinted in pain. He restrained himself from attacking physically. He approached the preacher, taking his right hand and licking his thumb, smearing a light coat of saliva on each of his fingertips. He walked in front of the preacher and lifted his head to meet his gaze. The preacher froze in place, stunned by the appearance of the stranger.

"Yes, my brother, I hear you," Pete replied as he reached up and gently touched the preacher's forehead with his right hand.

With their gazes still locked, Celesthargor tilted his head downward, revealing a hint of evil within him. He then darted off, disappearing out of view. The preacher began to shake off the incident that just occurred. A peculiar feeling overcame him as he returned to preaching. Soon an unexplainable lust slowly built up within him. He looked around and noticed a skimpy pink dress hugging well-defined butt cheeks on a nearby prostitute. Finding his lust growing stronger he turned to his right. A woman walked by him, but all he noticed were her huge well-developed breasts with erect nipples he thought to be the size of eraser heads pointing at a 45-degree angle. Sweat began to bead up on his brow and soak his underarms. He looked behind him and spotted a beautiful blonde with swollen, collagen-filled, "come screw me" red lips. Her tongue lustfully licked her upper lip, seeming to blow kisses as she passed by. There he saw a six-foot tall brunette wearing a leather garter and a spiked dog collar around her neck. Her hair hung to her waist. To her side stood a Great Dane on a leash with the same exact collar. She gently pushed the dog away as it licked her thigh. "Not now, Pookie," she replied. "Wait 'till we get home."

Just then, two men arm in arm walked out of the porno shop he stood in front of. As they passed, he noticed one reach down and grab the others butt. They made eye contact with the street priest and blew him a kiss. Unable to contain his lust, he flung aside his Bible and grabbed his crotch and rushed into the porno shop. He rushed up to the register, shaking and sweating with an uncontrollable primal urge. "Give me quarters. And can I have some of that masturbation sauce? Hurry up man, I don't have all day."

The drag queen behind the counter handed him the stuff and some paper towels. "Clean up after you're done."

He rushed to one of the back rooms slamming the door behind him.

TWENTY-FIVE

AS THE DARKNESS of night set in, shimmering stars filled the skies. Celesthargor shivered from both the cold and lack of nourishment. His host's lips were cracked and swollen; the saliva thickened in his mouth. He spotted a liquor store across the street from where he stood. Curiously, he entered the establishment heading straight for a rack of assorted candies. In a brutish manner, he grabbed two hands full of candies and, without opening the packages, shoved them into his mouth. He smeared the assorted chocolates across his face. Small chunks of chocolate clung to his mouth as he staggered to the nearby bottles of liquor.

A long-haired college student struggled to look over the aisles to see what the stranger was doing. Celesthargor grabbed a bottle of whiskey and unscrewed the cap. He consumed half the bottle in one gulp. He pulled the bottle from his lips, spitting in disgust. He threw the bottle across the store, sending it crashing into a beer display. He reached for the next bottle that happened to be a sweet liquor. The beast cautiously opened it and sniffed its content. Greeted by the sweet smell of peppermint, he greedily raised the bottle to his mouth and began to chug. A voice from behind the counter intruded halfway through the bottle. "Hey dude. You gonna pay for the stuff you ate, and those two bottles?"

When he finished drinking the contents of the bottle he glared at the storekeeper. With the aggressiveness of a baseball pitcher, he threw the empty bottle at the bewildered man. "What the," the keeper yelled as he tried to duck.

Unable to react in time, the bottle crashed into his elbow, leaving a deep gash, blood spurting from the wound as glass shattered everywhere. As he fell behind the counter, he hit the silent alarm. He then crawled through the broken glass into a corner behind the counter and waited, nursing his wound. Celesthargor turned his attention back to the bottles before him.

Sirens filled the night air around the store and within seconds the store was completely surrounded by squad cars. Six officers entered the establishment, three at a time. Two had shotguns and the rest wielded their department-issued 9mm Glocks. The lead officer aimed his gun at the possessed man. "Drop the bottle! Turn around and lock your hands behind your head!"

In a drunken stupor, Pete spun around to face the officers. With a devilish growl, he threw another bottle at the crowd of officers with great strength but without accuracy, almost striking the lead officer. "Holy shit!!! That was hard!" yelled one of the officers.

"Don't move or we'll shoot!" shouted the lead officer.

Ignoring the order, Pete reached for another bottle. "I said don't move asshole!" warned the lead again.

Just then, Pete launched the bottle with such force that he lost his balance, bracing himself as not to fall. This time the bottle was right on the money, smashing into the lead officer's face. Shattered glass blistered the officer's face, launching his body backward as his legs flung into the air. He landed with a thud on the back of his head, his gun sliding across the floor, leaving him unconscious. The demon laughed at the fallen man's plight, reaching for another bottle. The remaining officers cracked with anger, unloading every round from their guns. Massive fireballs emerged from the barrels followed by traces of unburned gun powder. As Pete was repeatedly struck, chunks of flesh flew from his body, spraying blood through the puffs of smoke. He slammed into some shelves nesting the liquor bottles, launched backward by the intense force of the impact, knocking them over and causing them to fold underneath his weight. As the smoke cleared, the officers cautiously approached him. Pete's legs began to shake violently as cops got closer to the fallen man. Without warning, a large blade erupted through Pete's chest. His chest cavity was forced apart and the demon launched upward with lizard-like agility. In mid-flight, it began to realign its joints and umbrella itself out. It landed, sprawled out on fallen shelves, crushing them even further beneath its feet.

Several of the officers opened fire. One of the officers holding a shotgun froze in place at the sight of the vile beast. Bullets ripped into the beast, but the wounds were quickly pulled shut by quivers of electricity. The officers backed out of the store trying to escape the vengeance of the Celesthargor. The one in shock was chosen to be the next victim. Unable to do anything else, he raised his shotgun to block the oncoming blade. The combination of stainless steel and synthetic plastic was no match for a blade that was sharp beyond all human comprehension. The blade caught him above the clavicle, the slicing right through his bullet proof vest and through his chest, cleaving him in two. Each side fell to the floor. Different colors of internal gelatin splashed onto the floor.

The beast turned and crashed through the doors of the liquor store to make its escape. He was greeted by a hail of bullets from more officers positioned outside behind their cars. Again, bluish bolts appeared where the holes had been ripped on the body of the beast. With an ear-piercing shriek, it leaped onto the roof of the closest squad car, causing the tires to explode. Using it as a stepping stone for the next vehicle, the beast moved with such speed that it seemed a blur. It jumped the wide gap between cars causing similar eruptions from the tires of each car, continuing until it reached the side of a building, that it scaled with ease.

Galvanized by the intense attack on their fellow officers, the remaining patrolmen regrouped into the undamaged squad cars and radioed for helicopter backup. As they began their pursuit, they heard the devilish screams of the beast as it ran from roof top to roof top. The officers combed the area with spotlights. Some of the officers lost their composure from what they just witnessed and the adrenaline rush surging through their bodies "It's here! It's over here!" one of the officers shouted.

Just as the majority of the squad turned their attention to the spotlight, the beast used its unnatural speed and agility to escape from view. Once again it was spotted, but before attention could be brought to it, it vanished again. An eager voice barks over the police scanner. "Damnit, HQ. Where is that chopper!"

A calm voice echoed in response. "Car 912, we're right above you! We are unable to locate suspect. We're gonna switch to infra-red."

After a brief pause, the voice called out again. "Attention dispatch, we are unable to locate suspect. He must be indoors cause he's not showing up on thermal imaging."

Just then a voice came over the band. "Eye in the sky, check your equipment. The suspect just passed right in front of us. We're right under you."

"Sorry, 912, all systems check out. The only thing coming out is your squad car."

Moments passed and no one else was able to report a sighting. It had managed to escape capture. An A.P.B. was put out on a large rabid animal of some sort. All were warned that it was extremely dangerous. Each officer was ordered to call for back up and approach with caution.

In the distance the beast could hear the chopper and the police sirens searching for it. Celesthargor was in a panic to find a new disguise. It crawled down a wall, peeking into a small window braced by wire bars. It saw a large white male sporting no hair, restrained by a straight-jacket. Two large male orderlies strapped him to a chair which was bolted to the floor. In front of him stood a tall, athletic brunette nurse with her skirt lifted to her waist, baring her ass to the restrained man. Waving it from side to side she looked at him mockingly. "Is this what you wanted from your victims?" She looked at the two orderlies. "Make sure he's tied down. I don't want him getting loose while you both do me at the same time."

There in a straight-jacket restrained by straps sat Little Tom. Little Tom had been committed to this mental ward because he had been incestuously molested and tortured as a child. The years of abuse left him a shell of a human being and mentally retarded. All he could do was seek revenge on the female gender. His crimes were so brutal that his victims were restrained to beds or wheelchairs and had to be fed intravenously for the remainder of their bleak lives. Due to the savageness of their injuries, these victims prayed each night that they would not wake up the following morning.

Little Tom appeared a bit of an oddity due to his large body, huge muscular arms, and small bald head. Even his appearance gave the impression that this individual did not belong in society.

Engaged by the sight of the striping nurse in front of him being fondled by the two orderlies that had restrained him only moments before, he began to whimper and rock from side to side. Tears of lust and rage ran down his face as the threesome came to a climax only a few feet from where he sat restrained. In the distance by the window the demon watched. It patiently waited for the nurse and two orderlies to finish and leave the room before he made his entrance.

CHAPTER

TWENTY-SIX

JOHNNY PUSHED THE food tray down the cold, white corridor, stopping at each room on his nightly dinner delivery for the patients. He first stopped at cell 301 calling out for the occupant to retrieve the tray of food. "Okay Bob. It's chow time. Come and get it. Sorry, but no cobbler tonight."

This scene was repeated down the hall until Johnny reached Little Tom's cell. "Okay 304. Got your favorite tonight. Macaroni and cheese and some yummy apple sauce. Come and get it."

Johnny placed the tray by the slit on the door expecting the familiar wart-covered hands to greedily reach out and pull the tray into the room. After several moments of silence, Johnny stated in a sarcastic manner, "What's wrong buddy? Macaroni is your favorite. Don't tell me you're on a diet."

Several more seconds passed. Johnny grew worried. "Tom? C'mon Tom! Stop playin' around. This isn't funny anymore."

Still no response. He decided to take a peek inside. Seeing nothing through the looking glass he cautiously opened the door, prepared for a surprise attack. Still nothing happened. He then ventured further in. To his disbelief, in the center of the room lay a mangled

136

chair and straight jacket ripped to shreds. He looked to the left to find the safety window had been forced in. He rushed to the emergency button and punched it. Sirens sounded and emergency lights flashed red, draping the walls in brilliant crimson. Out on the sidewalk, a large figure disappeared into the shadows.

✳   ✳   ✳

Back at the lab, Michelle frantically conducted tests in hopes of identifying the perpetrator of her nephew's murder. Tired and frustrated she became careless and dropped a test tube onto the floor.

"Ahh Damn't" she screamed as she pounded on the table. Bobby Lee tried to comfort her. "It's okay Michelle. It's nothing but a 25-cent test tube. You're strung out. You need a break. I know a place just down the street. Let's go and have a drink."

"SCREW YOU BOBBY!!! This thing is out there killing people and children and you have the audacity to keep hitting on me."

Bobby stood there, partially stunned. "Whoa Barbie babe. I might be head over heels crazy about you, but I surely know the difference of when and where to hit on you. I'm just trying to ease the pain you're goin through."

"Damnit, Bobby, I'm sorry. I didn't mean to snap at you. It's not your fault. It's just that I have nothing to go by on this case and it pisses me off."

"Ya know something. I've never heard you cuss before... and you know what else? It becomes you." He leaned over and gave her a hug.

"Thanks Bobby! I needed that. You know, underneath all that hair and tattoos you're really a bleeding heart, and I love that about you. But right now, I need to find this thing. It killed someone very special in my life and I need to stop it."

"I understand. How about I get us something to eat. My treat. Only one condition. You have to promise me that you'll take a little break and eat." "Okay, okay" she replied.

She took a deep breath and turned her attention back to her work. Her focus turned to an evidence bag containing the contents that belonged to her nephew. Opening it, she spilled the contents onto a table. She picked up the ring and gazed at it, remembering the joyous occasion when she, Jesse and his parents were having a picnic at a local park. She vividly remembered when both she and her nephew planted a small tree in the name of their family. It was then that she had given him this ring as a late birthday present. She remembered the warm smile and hug that he gave her when she gave him the gift. "As long as you wear this ring, I will always be with you," she told him. "You will never be alone." Tears filled her eyes and she had a sudden urge to return to the park.

It was a beautiful night. The smell of rain still filled the air even though it had not sprinkled in several hours. A cool, refreshing breeze passed over Michelle's skin as she reached into her pocket to remove the ring. She passed several swing sets and walked toward a small clearing where a single, small tree stood out. She knelt down to bury the ring. "You will always live in my heart and I will never forget you. We will miss you very much. Someday we will meet again."

She decorated the tree with a beautiful fluorescent pink bow she pulled from her pocket. The sound of someone whimpering broke the silence of the moment. She turned and looked at the bushes behind her, unaware of the danger that hid in their shadows. As she turned back to what she was doing, a grotesque wart-covered hand pulled apart the branches of a bush to better see the gorgeous figure before him. Little Tom heart raced as he pulled his diseased member out of his pants and began to pet it, his mind filled with the lustful images of his host. With each stroke he became more and more enraged. His anxiety built as he constantly replayed the scenes of the torturous sex acts performed before him while he was restrained in the county mental ward. His heart beat and his whimpering became faster. Sweat covered his bald, tapered head. His nose flared as snot as thick as tree sap spilled out of his nostrils.

Unable to contain himself any longer, he dashed silently into a full-fledged sprint. A strange feeling passed over Michelle, causing her to look up. Seeing nothing she continued to sob. Suddenly to her surprise, a huge, wart-infested hand reached under her left arm raking across her chest. Before she could get off a scream, a second hand covered her mouth, launching her helplessly into the air. Carried a short distance to a secluded area she was thrown face first into the soft grass. As her face was driven into the mud by a series of heavy blows to the back of her head. It wasn't long until she lost consciousness.

With raw strength and lustful rage, Little Tom ripped her pants and undergarments off in one clean stroke. He pulled her up to her knees, face still down in the grass, and began to ram his member deep in her rectum. After several moments he flipped her over to reveal her bleeding, mud-caked face. This was not about the physical relief that comes with such an act. The demon knew this woman was somehow related to his old enemy P'an Ku. He could smell the faint stench of the old angel on her soul. He would take any opportunity to make the old holy man suffer, as well as all those that followed him. He looked down at the blood-soaked face of his victim. A serpentine tongue licked at her now broken jaw. He shoved his member hard between her legs, thrusting faster and faster, enjoying the sensation in his groin. After exploding deep inside her, he rested his 390-pound frame on his victim and began to chuckle.

TWENTY-SEVEN

JOE SAT QUIETLY in the darkness of his house. His meditation was broken by the ringing of his cell phone. As Joe picked up the phone and began to speak, his face became flushed. He grabbed his keys and ran outside to his car. He fumbled for a moment trying to get the key into the ignition, then peeled out of his driveway and sped off toward the hospital. The news that his soon to be bride was being airlifted to the city hospital made his heart sink to his stomach and his nerves bundle almost to the point where he lost control of his vehicle. His car spun around and white smoke filled the air as his tires lost traction. The vehicle came to rest on the side of the road. "Get a grip, Joe. You're not going to do her any good dead."

He shook off the anger and sped off toward the hospital.

*　*　*

The emergency doors of the hospital exploded open as a broken Michelle was sped to emergency surgery. On the stretcher she looked inhuman. Patches of hair had been pulled from her head, grass caked in with a combination of dried blood and mud covered the side of her face clogging one nostril, coating her gums and teeth. The doctors worked frantically to save her knowing that she had lost a lot of blood. It was a very touch and go situation. Timing was critical.

As Joe entered the parking lot of the hospital, he slammed on the brakes causing his tires to screech. As he came to a stop, he flung the car door open. Wasting no time he ran into the emergency waiting room, searching for anyone who could give him information about his bride. Down the hall he found Steve and Christine. Steve was embracing Christine as she buried her head in Steve's chest, sobbing hysterically. Joe approached them. "What's going on? What happened?"

Unable to respond, Christine continued to sob. Steve sat his wife down and walked over to Joe. "Joe, I think it would be best if you had a seat."

"I'm fine just where I am. What the hell is going on?" Joe asked angrily.

"Joe. Michelle has been attacked. We don't know the extent of the damage. The doctor should be out shortly."

Just then a door opened and the doctor walked out. "I need to speak to the immediate family members only." The doctor then turned his attention to Joe.

"Who are you?"

"I'm her fiancée," Joe replied.

"Oh. So, you're the father then."

Joe looked puzzled. "What? Father? Father of what?"

"Then I take it you didn't know that she was a few months pregnant," the doctor asked.

Joe, still too stunned to respond just stood there.

"Well. It's still too early to tell whether or not we can save the baby. All we can do now is pray."

"What about Michelle?" Joe asked.

"She has fallen into a coma and it will be a little while before she can have any visitors. There is a cafeteria down the hall and to the right. If you want any refreshments, you can get them down there. Please just stay calm. I'll let you know if anything changes."

The doctor left as Joe dropped onto a nearby chair, stunned by what he had just heard. Christine and Steve followed suit and sat in silence.

*　　*　　*

The sunset blanketed the city as the nightlife on the street picked up. P'an Ku was in a local convenience store. A young boy stood near the candy display eating what appeared to be a large sugar ball. Watching the satisfaction spread over the boy's face as he consumed the candy, P'an Ku became curious and wanted to try out this new, wonderful cuisine. Looking for a similar package he found it and purchased it. Leaving the store he opened the package, sniffed it, shrugged his shoulders and consumed it. He smiled at a small child and her mother as they walked past him. Within moments his eyes widened with surprise as the small, white tablet began to foam uncontrollably. His cheeks swelled, foam seeping between his lips. Not able to contain the pressure any longer he opened his mouth while staring directly at a small girl and began to yell. Caught by surprise, the angel dropped the package he thought was something sweet.

The sight of the strange man foaming at the mouth, yelling hysterically caused the young girl to panic and she herself began to scream. The girl's mother, fearing an attack began to scream for help while slugging P'an Ku with her purse. Embarrassed by this encounter he ran off. After cleaning himself off he snickered to himself. He looked at the package in his hand. "What in God's name is a seltzer tablet and how can these kids eat this garbage?" he chuckled. As he wiped the remains of foam from his mouth, he realized that he must have looked like a wild man.

Just then, a familiar smell like no other coated his nostrils. He stopped in his tracks and began to sniff the air as he scanned the crowd. Unable to locate the direction of the smell and fearful of a surprise attack that may endanger the surrounding people, he quickly backed into an alley, placing his back against a wall. With his back to the wall, he scanned the sea of people near the alley. Sticking out like a sore thumb stood a 6'9", 350-pound monstrosity. As the Frankenstein Ish man walked closer and closer, P'an Ku remained unnaturally calm. He could smell the demonic beast hiding within the freakish man before him. How fitting that Celesthargor choose such an outcast to host his vile entity. He was prepared for the battle at hand; sure, it would be his last. He remembered the premonition he had when he first sensed his mortal enemy, and he was right. The demon had become more powerful than even he thought possible. P'an Ku knew he was only there to buy Joe a little more time to come to terms with what he must do.

As their eyes magnetized onto each other, the tendons and veins on Little Tom's neck and bold head flared. Looking into P'an Ku's soul, the demon realized that over time he had grown extremely more powerful than his age-old adversary. As he passed, they broke eye contact. Little Tom turned into a dark alley. Knowing he must, P'an Ku followed. Reaching a dead end, the beast mechanically turned to meet his pursuer. A dark, heavy, intelligent voice filled the alley, sobering a drunken bum sleeping within a cardboard house. "P'an Ku, my old and trusty adversary. I knew you would show. When and where was not important. I had longed to see you for once we were best of friends. Do you remember, before my King was cast down? We had a bond that no one would understand. You were always the stronger of us. Now the tables have turned. I can see in your eyes that

I am the stronger. Once I rid the path of you my destiny will be complete. My king, The One True God, will make his presence known on this earth. Personally, I don't see what he wants these pitiful souls for. But I am but a soldier. My will is not my own."

P'an Ku looked staunchly at Celesthargor. "My old friend, you are right. We were once true friends. However, my will is of my own. That makes me stronger. Even if I lose, do you think that I am the only one that is sent to stop you? There is another. One that is surprisingly stronger and he will prevail. I am prepared to die. I am nothing more than a sacrificial lamb. You may destroy me, but my soul will never die. I will only be sent back to something that you seek but will never, NEVER have. True love. Something your King is incapable of giving."

That response stung Celesthargor. "Enough talk!" he growled. "Your destiny ends here and now."

They both positioned their bodies in offensive stances. Each cautiously approached one another waiting for the other to attack. With a quick burst of power, the fight had started. Celesthargor shot like a rocket toward P'an Ku with agility and speed. This caught P'an Ku by surprise and he was launched into a brick wall. In midair P'an Ku was able to recover and caught the wall with his feet, propelling himself back to his adversary. He attacked with a strike to Celesthargor' face. Celesthargor was able to redirect the blow, sending P'an Ku across the alley into trash and empty boxes. Celesthargor looked to his left and spotted a metal pipe about four feet in length. He grinned as he picked it up.

Recovering, P'an Ku picked himself up and spun to face the demon. Celesthargor quickly attacked and swung the pipe to P'an Ku's face. Still groggy from the fall he was unable to react properly and the pipe did its job, landing on P'an Ku's forearm and completely crushing it. P'an Ku's right arm dangled from his side, shattered and useless. The pain shot through his body almost sending the angel out of its host. Celesthargor did not waste the moment. After crushing P'an Ku's arm, he quickly swung the pipe downward at P'an Ku's right knee, crunching and folding it outward. Celesthargor instantly spun around and smashed P'an Ku's left leg at the kneecap, folding it outward. P'an Ku was now standing on the nubs of his knees, both legs crushed by his attacker. Celesthargor attacked the angel's face with stone hands launching P'an Ku into the air. P'an Ku flew feet over head into the boxes behind him, landing face first into the soft card board. His breathing stopped. Moments later two bursts of energy emerged from his body. Both spirits entwined as one and were launched to the heavens. "That was too easy," Celesthargor laughed as he left the ally.

CHAPTER
TWENTY-EIGHT

SLUMPED OVER A chair in the hospital, Joe had fallen asleep. As he slept, P'an Ku entered his dream. "My student, my friend, I am afraid that I will not be by your side when you face the demon. Mind what you have learned, for the beast is very powerful. Although I will not be by your side physically, I will be with you. The power I brought with me to your realm is now yours. Remember, the purity of your heart is a power the beast cannot compete with. Turn to your love for strength and you will be victorious."

With those last words, P'an Ku faded away. Abruptly Joe awoke. He almost jumped out of his chair, catching himself at the last moment. His heart raced. He knew that P'an Ku was gone. The fact that his soon to be wife had been attacked and left for dead, coupled with the fact that he knew that his master was gone, he felt a surge of strength flow through his blood. Enraptured by the swelling of his body from the energy that grew inside him, he thought back to his training and was reminded of what was now happening to him.

A nurse approached the group. "You can see her now, but please only one at a time."

Joe agreed and bolted to her side. He sat down in a chair near the bed and held her hand. He stared at her face and caressed her forehead. "Baby you're going to be okay. The doctor says you're going to be fine. Hang in there."

As he held her hand he looked up to the ceiling. "I know you're there. And I know what you want me to do, but please, PLEASE don't take her away from me."

He was distracted by two male orderlies just outside the room. The two were talking about Michelle, unaware that someone could hear the conversation.

"Yup, it's sad. We got another coma patient. I don't know what they're saying about her but I'll bet you lunch that by the end of the week they are burying her."

The other orderly looked up at his friend. "You're on. I owe you dinner anyway for the last one so this ought to give me a chance to break even." They walked away.

Joe's heart sank into his stomach and he started to cry. He lifted his head and looked straight forward, staring blankly into the wall. Tears of rage filled his eyes. "DEMON, HEAR ME NOW! IT'S TIME TO DIE!"

As he stood up focused on what he must now do, his mind was filled with memories of his deceased instructor telling him, "Not only will you fight it, but you will seek it out. It will have taken everything that you love and destroyed it. You will do everything in your power to kill it. Even if it means death. Remember we all have a time to die."

Joe took one last look at his beloved Michelle. Rage filled his heart as his focus turned to the beast that took his happiness and left the hospital.

✳　✳　✳

Slight whispers could be heard throughout the church as Father McNelly refilled the urns with newly blessed holy water. He filled each urn, blessing them one more time. In the process, he heard the hushed whisper of a familiar voice in prayer. Out of curiosity he scanned the church, spotting Joe Jeager kneeling down on a pew at the front of the church. With concern Father McNelly approached and adjusted his robe as he knelt next to his life-long friend. He turned to Joe. "I haven't seen you in a long time. What brings you to church?"

Joe turned trying to hide the apprehension in his eyes, sweat glistening on the rim of his scalp. With a keen eye, McNelly easily felt the fear in Joe's eyes. He firmly placed his hand on Joe's forearm. "Talk to me. Talk to me, Joe. I know something is wrong. Look at me. You know me better than anyone else." "Well father..., "Joe began.

Abruptly Father McNelly interrupted. "Enough with this father stuff. Call me what you used to call me."

Joe's eyes widened as he says sarcastically, "Oh really?"

Father McNelly chuckled. "Wait a minute! Not that! Call me Billy." They both chuckled for a moment.

"No, really Joe. What's the problem?"

Joe looked straight into Father McNelly eyes and paused. "Do you really want to know what's going on?"

"Yes, I do."

"Okay, to make a long story short, here's the deal. An angel chose me to be the champion of earth. He's trained me is some freak ass style of fighting I have never seen or heard of. He told me there is a beast out there that I must confront, and I'm not talking about some big drunk asshole, Father McNelly. I mean a real demon, sent by Satan and what not. It has taken everything I love and is prepared to open a path for Satan's reign. Now it is time for me to go get the son-of-a-bitch, even if it means my life. But I'm scared, Billy. Scared beyond belief. This thing has survived for over four thousand years. What makes me think that I can stop it? The angle said so, that's why. I've come here to yell at God for choosing me and yet ask for his help. Am I confused or what?" Joe paused and looked to see his friend's reaction.

Father McNelly paused for a moment, not knowing what to say. He turned to his friend with a puzzled look. "It is time, isn't it? The King of Darkness has sent a messenger. Doomsday is near and you have been chosen to try and save us. The Church has been aware of this prophecy for some time, but I had no idea you were the one."

Joe looked, shrugging his shoulders, saying in a slight arrogant tone, "Something like that... but why me? Of all the people in the world, why did he choose someone like me, someone who has given up his faith. He has taken everything that I loved and he expects me to be his hero? Why the hell did he do this to me? I am not some super hero leaping tall buildings in a single bound, ready to save the day. I'm just a man trying to put his life back together, trying to find a piece of happiness in the shitty hand I was dealt."

In a confident voice Father McNelly stated, "Look, it's time for me to tell you the truth. There was a reason why I was so mean to you. For the most part I was just a mean kid, so I picked on everyone. But with you I was jealous. There was always something about you that I envied. I couldn't pinpoint it but it was there, staring me in the face every day. You are special Joe. You are very special. It is like your grandmother said the night that changed my life forever. I'll admit she scared the living crap out of me."

Father McNelly made the sign of the cross, realizing his language was not proper for a man of the cloth. He composed himself and turned back to Joe. "It was the night at your house. She pointed to you and had you touch that crystal on her cane. The color didn't change but instead it lit up like a light bulb. She told you it was because your soul was good and strong. She then kissed your cheek and said, 'This is your calling. You were born for this reason. You are the ONE!'

Believe it or not I never forgot a single word she said that night. It changed me as you can see. I should have known you were the liberator the prophecy spoke of."

Joe, you need to know that I have chosen to leave the Catholic faith. Joe replied "what? Why? Why are you leaving the church? Father McNelly replied "I knew this was going to shock and scare you especially now because of what you are going through! But I want to assure you my faith in the Lord Jesus Christ is absolutely rock solid! Now more then every! However, the Rome Catholic Church will NOT! Allow me to share this important secret knowledge that desperately need to get out to the people. The Catholic Church has become Luciferic! Yes, I said Luciferic! And I would really like to share the information with you. This information will help you in your relationship with the Father in Heaven.

Can I share this information with Joe? Joe replied "sure I would like to hear it" "but after, I'm got to ask you for a favor" Sure, I will help you in any way I can.

First, you need to know that all of us who has taken a human body are the fallen Angels! Yes, we are! Are heavenly Father, love us and has given us "Free Will" Lucifer however, had lied to us, the angels, saying things like we could do what we wanted here on Earth, and God the Father would not be able to see our sins down here. And through free will, and like naive little children, we believed him and came down here to have all kinds of sex, a playground so to speak. And once our body dies the deal was that Lucifer gets you soul. Now, what the people don't know is that we have been merged together with a demon inside the human body. This is known as "parthenogenesis". Science says it a reptilian part of our brain, but it's not.

Are you still with me, Joe? Joe nodes his head "yes" and listening intensely. Okay, then listen closely, your eyes are the windows to the pit and to the Heavenly Father. Yes, they are! The right eye is linked to God in Heaven and the left eye is linked to a worm in the pit. The worm from the pit knows the Bible better then anyone on Earth, it has to be if it wants your soul for its eternal food. And the right eye is also seeing your sins as well, however it watches for your repentance and confession of your sins and acceptance of his son Jesus Christ as Lord and savior who has taken your punishment for you on the cross for your disobedience. Once Jesus becomes your Lord and savior, the connection to the pit is severed and all your sins are wiped clean and can never be used against you. Both your eyes will have now become one, and filled with the light of God.

I also want to ask you Joe, why is the building of the Vatican in the shape of a snake wearing a crown? And it's given birth to another snake. If you look straight down onto the Vatican building it's also looks like an upside down cross going into a key hole? The cross represented the condition we are in once we a born into these meat suits. To understand what is happening you must have the keys to heaven. What do you do with keys? You put them into a lock and turn it upside-down to unlock it! Joe, you have to turn the world upside-down to see what is going on. You will see symbolism all over the Vatican and Churches, court houses, Law office, everywhere. This is the information all these Luciferians clubs like the Freemasons, or the Skull and Bones, or Illuminati have on the people! They mock you and me by putting the all-seeing-eye on our money knowing we would never know what it means.

Joe, are you aware that these negative people in those so call clubs are telling many truths through there movies. Yes, they are, have you seen the movie, Alien? The creature called a Xenomorph! It has a tale like a scorpion and its skeletal system is on the outside of it body like an insect. Lucifer is the King of the Locus, King of the bugs. These is one of the things that will be waiting for those who have not found Jesus! And it will be a whole lot worse than any movie can ever make. Joe, go on the internet when you can and watch and listen to the Catholic Church prayers, you will be shocked to see they are praying to Lucifer not Jesus Christ!

Joe, looks at Father McNelly, Wow! Then how do we save ourselves? What do I need to do?

Father McNelly replied "All you have to do is turn the world upside-down and see what it really is, turn to Jesus and apologies for all your sins, and repent and ask Jesus to come into your host body. Do this with you whole heart and the connection to the pit will be severed. Both eyes become one with Lord, and you will be saved at the time of your death.

Father McNelly, ask Joe too look at a statue of Lady Justice we happen to have in my church. It was here before I arrived. I want you to look at it! Can you tell me what it's telling the people? Joe looked at it for a moment and shook his head and said "no" "I have no idea"

Father McNelly told Joe first, you have to know what the original looked like, you can find this information in Torah Cards books. Yes, this was part of my studies before Joe gave him a smart remark. When you go to the Lady Justice page of the book you will see a picture of Lady Justice standing holding a sword with her arm straight up pointing to the heavens and the scales of Justice is held at waist level. When you read what this means you will find that the sword represents the people, and the tip of the sword represents the voice of the people, and the scales of justice is only there to interpret the laws the people have written to govern themselves and that's it. Now after hearing this information and looking at the statue of Lady Justice in my church, what do you think it trying to tell you?

Joe, looked at it and said "The sword is pointing to the ground which it telling me the people don't matter here"

Father McNelly replied "Yes, very good, what else do you see?"

Joe, replied "I see the tip of the sword pointing to the ground and that tells me that the people have no voice here!"

"Excellent! Joe" Father McNelly shouted.

"What else do you see" He asked.

Joe response was "I see the scales of Justice is above everything else and that tells me that the court system here are more important than the people! And they will make up laws that suit themselves"

"Fantastic Joe, do you see anything else?"

"Joe replied, I see the Lady Justice is wearing a blind fold, that tells me that you will not get a fair trial here and no justice! For justice is blind."

Yes, Father McNelly replied "this is what I meant about turning the world upside-down and see the world for what is really going on.

Joe, you now hold the keys to heaven, the mind of Christ!

Joe replied "that was a lot to absorb, but it really makes sense to me." "I will pray and repent and afterward I will need a favor from you." Would that be, okay?

Father McNelly said yes that would be okay, and gave Joe some private time to be with the Lord.

After some time had passed Joe Walk up to Father McNelly and asked.

Father, I need that favor now.

Of course, what can I do for you? Father McNelly asked.

Well, it's really two favors?" Joe asked.

Father McNelly looked at him again with a puzzled look. "Okay. What are they?"

"One. I need for you to really pray for me, and pray hard. And two, I need some holy water. About a quart or so."

"Of course I'll pray for you. I will stay up all night praying for you. And as for your second request…" "Father McNelly lifted a large jug and filled it from the main fountain by an altar." "Is this enough?"

Joe grinned. He grabbed the jug and commenced to fill some balloons. After taking what he needed of the holy water, he then hugged

Father McNelly and whispered, "Thank you for the wonderful talk!" He turned and walked towards the door, heading for home. "Joe, wait a minute" Father McNelly called out. "I have something for you I believe you will need it." He walked into a back room and within minutes Father McNelly emerged with three ounces of anointed olive oil, from the Mount of Olives at Gethsemani. "Joe" Father McNelly stated. "This is very special oil; it comes from the garden where Jesus Christ has taken the sins of the world upon himself." "Why give it to me?" Joe asked. "It will help you in your time of need, just listen to the little voice talking to now. Learn to trust it, it's the voice from the Father in Heaven. And it will tell you when to use it" Father McNelly replied. Joe placed the glass vile into a small velvet black bag with a draw string and packed it with holy water he had collected. "Thank you for everything" Joe stated. "Go and do whatever you must, and know this, God and the Angels from heaven are with you." Joe smiles at Father McNelly and leaves to prepare for the confrontation.

TWENTY-NINE

ONCE HOME, HE changed into black pants and a black T-shirt, sporting special boxing shoes that he had rigged with razor blades covered in black shoe polish strategically placed on the outer edges of his feet. The bottoms of the blades were coated with a rubber cocking to silence his steps. He strapped a leather sheath across his back, hosting a pair of custom-made Brat Jum Do, also known as butterfly swords. He placed several pieces of PVC piping, 4 inches in length and an inch and a half in diameter onto a cloth laid out on a kitchen table. He placed the balloons into each tube. He then placed them strategically on his belt. Joe placed the anointed oil given to him by Father McNelly into a balloon as well and into its own PVC pipe and marked the word oil on it. He then placed it in his right pocket away from the other tubes.

Stepping into his souped up, customized sports car, he revs the engine slightly to warm it up. Realizing he needed gas; he took off to a nearby convenience store. At the counter he noticed three men coming into the store wearing masks. One of the thugs was holding a 45 caliber semi-automatic pistol. The other two had a knife and a machete. Joe tossed his cash on the counter and looked at the clerk. And spoke. "Can you catch?"

The store clerk nodded, "Yeah, why?"

Without a word, Joe spun around to face the gun-wielding bandits. "Hey man, everything is cool. It's all yours. No one needs to get hurt here."

At that moment he knew that his senses had changed somehow. Smelling the marijuana in their sweat coupled with the distinct scent of cocaine, he knew he had the advantage. His keen sense of hearing picked up the mechanisms of the gun as the thug fingered the trigger, knowing exactly when the hammer would be released giving him further advantage.

He waited for the proper moment, and WHAM! There it was.

The bandit holding the machete stepped within kicking range of his razor covered feet. BOOM!! He exploded like a flick of a switch. A fine-tuned killing machine emerged. The gun was swiftly smacked out of the perpetrator's hand and tossed behind Joe towards the clerk. Standing in a goofy manner was the helpless store clerk, having no knowledge of how to operate the handgun that he had just caught.

After relieving the assailant of his gun, Joe immediately struck the knee of the second assailant wielding the knife with a low kick. As the man fell forward, Joe smashed the bandit in the nose, sending him flying over his machete-wielding partner. Joe's senses were so heightened the last thug seemed to move in slow motion as he attacked. As the man swung the machete down, Joe shifted his body, striking the man's elbow upward with one hand while striking the man's wrist downward with the other, snapping his forearm in two, sending the bone piercing through the skin. Continuing the attack with an elbow strike, Joe smashed his attacker's hand, shoving the fractured bone deep into the attacker's throat, killing him instantly.

Joe looked around seeing all of his assailants down. He brushed himself off and left, telling the clerk to keep the change. Before exiting he noticed to his right a store camera. Knowing that the events that had taken place were caught on tape, he smiled at the camera and walked out, mentally preparing himself for the events that were soon to take place.

His hair whipped in the wind as he drove along in his convertible. A small gust of wind blew across Joe's face carrying with it a smell so overbearing and vile that it stung the membranes of his nostrils causing his eyes to water. At first it was so pungent that he sought to escape it. Then, like the hunger of a savage wolf, he could not will the desire away to seek it out. He knew it was the thing he sought.

Following the stench, he turned into a city garage and parked. He exited his car and looked around the scent grew stronger as he came closer to a stairwell leading down to a lower floor restricted to employee personnel only. As he reached the bottom of the stairwell, the dank wetness of the concrete and the smell of rancid fuel caused the hair on his neck to stand. He continued further into the darkness. A swarm of flies filled the room as he noticed another vile stench. No longer masked by old fuel and oil the hideous stench of death hung in the air, pulling him further into the darkness. His face brushed across something soft and furry. Jumping with anxiety he flailed at it. It quickly wrapped around his arm. Joe jerked back quickly and a light clicked on. Joe sighed with relief realizing it was nothing more than a string to an overhead light. He had to squint as he waited for his eyes to adjust to the powerful glow. As the view before him came into focus, his jaw dropped. Slumped in a corner impaled on a mop handle that stuck several inches out of her mouth, was a young, bloated, female corpse. Maggots covered one eye socket as flies nested in her nostrils. Even more disgusting was that chunks of flesh had been bitten out of her. Where breasts used to be, mounds of torn flesh remained, ravaged by unforgiving teeth. Joe noticed that the carnage inflicted on the corpse had to have been done over a period of several days. He noticed a large boil surrounded by several other small blisters just underneath the woman's left breast. The skin over the boil peeled away in a slow manner as the milky lymph juices drained down her chest. Small spurts of rancid blood flew into the air, coating Joe's tongue. He gagged, pissed off at himself for standing there with his mouth gawking at the horrid scene. The strange taste of decaying flesh attacked his taste buds. He reeled in disgust and began to spit as knots built in his stomach.

Almost to the point of throwing up, his attention was drawn away by the thud of heavy footsteps. It sounded like steal crushing against a concrete floor. Joe looked around trying to find the source. The echo from the garage made it hard to pinpoint the location of the intruder. Frantically scanning his surroundings, Joe's eyes found a large figure hidden in the shadows just beyond the range of the lamp. Standing at the stairwell blocking his only means of escape stood the 390-pound 6'9" Goliath. Joe fiercely moved toward the wall of flesh. He was confident knowing that he now possessed the skills needed to overcome the largest of adversaries. He showed no fear.

Joe's rage took full control of his actions. "You vile son of a bitch. Kiss your ass goodbye."

"P'an Ku said there would be another, but I see he has wasted his time, and mine. You are nothing more than a feeble child. No match for a god like myself."

Joe grew silent knowing that this was the beast he had sought after. "Hell, I thought you'd be bigger. You ain't shit. I've destroyed bigger pieces of crap than you."

"You think so? I destroyed your teacher without breaking a sweat. P'an Ku fought like that bitch on the mop. Are you a bitch, Joe? Your Michelle was my bitch, and a sorry one at that! Maybe you'll be my little bitch? Once I've broken you, I'll do your ass like I did your swine of a woman!" The demon stared at his foe and laughed. "I think you'll make a good one! Gender makes no difference to me."

Rage filled Joe's heart. With hate taking over his actions, he charged Celesthargor. With his left hand he lunged to punch Pete's face. The demon countered by blocking it. Joe did not resist it but used the power to his advantage. He looped his hand in a continuous flow of force, stinging Celesthargor across the right side of the face. This distracted him just long enough to inflict a catastrophic blow to Celesthargor 's sternum, completely folding his entire chest. Joe stood back as the body before him began to tremble. Celesthargor had had enough. No more games. It was time to face his foe as his true self. No more hiding in these weak human bodies.

Blades ripped through the skin coming from different angles of the body. It didn't take long for the beast to tear through the feeble flesh of his host, revealing the true face of death. Joe reeled back in shock. Emerging before him was a four-armed, four-legged reptilian figure. Its scream and dancing pectorals sent a chill down Joe's spine. The sight of Celesthargor filled Joe with such fear. He knew he was facing a demon, but he was not prepared for the devilish figure that unfolded before him. Realizing that he was not prepared to battle this harbinger of death, he sought a means of escape. He knew that the blocked stairwell was his only means of escape. He would have to fight to the death to reach the exit. Reaching back with his left hand, he pulled both swords from their sheath, tossing one to his other hand.

In an orchestrated performance, the demon's blades of doom reached their pinnacle as he readied for attack. Joe struck at his foe before the monstrosity could setup on him. He knew this was the only chance he would have to flee. With an extreme burst of energy, he ran toward the foul beast. He leaped, slashing at every available limb blocking and cutting simultaneously. Using the beast's appendages as a ladder, Joe leaped from right to left, slicing the demon's pectorals and anything else he could reach. The attack was so viscous that one of the arms was left dangling by a mockery of flesh.

Flipping himself over the right shoulder of the beast, he brought one of the blades straight back down into its clavicle. Joe staggered to the stairwell turning quickly to survey the damage. He watched in horror as the lacerations were cauterized by electrical bolts, pulling the wounds together. Knowing now that he could not destroy this beast, he bolted up the stairs, leaping three at a time. At the top of the stairs, he looked down the center of the stairwell to see the reptilian head of the savage warrior staring back at him, grinning fiendishly. It began its ascent upward, all its arms and legs reaching for the railings for any support it could find. To his surprise, Joe found that the beast flowed like water up the tube-shaped center of the stair casing. Joe, now fearing for his life ran toward a row of cars. He looked back to see that the beast had just made it to his location.

Wasting no time, he jumped onto the roofs of several cars, running toward his only possible exit. The cars, representing only a slight hindrance to Celesthargor, were swept aside. Each upper limb reached for a vehicle, flipping them out of the way. Joe felt the cars being pulled from under his feet as he jumped from car to car. He glimpsed back and saw the beast on the tips of his heels. He lunged forward with his arms flailing into the air about twenty-five feet through an opening in the city parking garage, landing in a drainage ditch. The runoff in the drainage pipe swept Joe off his feet. He slid approximately three hundred feet into the underground sewage system.

THIRTY

RECOVERING FROM HIS fall, Joe managed to grab a nearby rail. He pulled himself up to the ledge of the ditch and ran ahead, fearing the beast was still in pursuit. He came upon a ladder which led him to the city streets above. He cursed under his breath at his former teacher as he climbed the ladder. "God damn't, P'an Ku. Ya never prepared me for this Fucken thing." 'Save the world' you said. 'Be a hero' you said. You son of a bitch! Why didn't you tell me what this thing really was?!"

He removed the manhole cover and cautiously peeked out. Surveying the surrounding area, he realized that the manhole opened up into a small alley. He lifted the cover and stepped out, feeling a little more confident he was safe.

Peeking over the edge of the building were the feral eyes and a mouth full of drool. As it spotted Joe, it launched into the air toward his victim. It slammed into the ground, causing it to quake and buckle underneath its weight. It lifted its frame back into attacking position.

Realizing that he lost one of his swords, Joe postured himself in a way to defend against the massive blows that rocketed toward him. He intercepted the first blow from the mammoth blades, but was thrown onto his back by the fierce attack. The beast laughed as it commenced to impale him with its huge talons. Doing his best to avoid the bone crushing blows, he skillfully redirected the massive power headed toward him, simultaneously slashing unmercifully with Joe's razor blade covered fighting shoes at the creature's legs, leaving a reign of electricity dancing across its skin.

Joe tried to roll away, but miscalculated his escape route, falling back into the uncovered manhole. Celesthargor seized the moment and stomped viscously at Joe, catching him in the chest. The force of the impact drove him through the hole. As Joe fell, one of his arms slammed in between the steps of the ladder, wrenching it out of its socket. The excruciating pain sent a paralyzing jolt through his body, causing him to howl in pain. Joe hit the ground with an unceremonious splash.

Joe quickly jumped back to his feet he began to run, holding his now useless arm and doing his best to ignore the pain that seared through his entire body. He ran to the next ladder that leads to another exit. Holding his breath, he slammed his shoulder into the ladder, unsuccessfully trying to reset his shoulder. New spikes of pain raked through his body as he reeled back. The shrieking scream of the demon sent a shot of adrenaline through his veins.

"Aggggghhhh!!!!" Joe yelled. "GODDAMNIT!!!!" He slammed his shoulder against the ladder again, this time the joint popped in from the impact. A slight sigh of relief fell over his face and he scurried up the ladder to make his escape. Still babying his weakened limb, he climbed out of the manhole onto the street. By his third step an explosion behind him sent asphalt rocketing toward his body. Raising both hands to shield his face, the shards of stone cut deep into numerous areas of his body, tearing both clothes and flesh.

The beast again showed itself, this time knowing that its adversary had no weapons or any means of protection. It knew it had the upper hand and was ready to take full advantage of it. The creature retracted its blades, intent on administering torturous blows to its prey, increasing the endorphin levels in its victim's body. Knowing that skill was no longer needed, the demon began to savagely pound on his weakened foe.

Joe tried all he could to deflect the monstrous attacks. Each blow came more forceful than the last. Fear gave way to frustration as he realized his end was near. "I'm sorry, Master. I was not strong enough to do what you asked of me," he thought to himself. Tears welled up in his eyes as he began to accept his fate.

Savoring the squeals of agony, the demon menacingly chuckled. He stepped back from his helpless victim, laughing at the mockery he made of his adversary's chosen student. Joe dragged his body up from the pavement, his mouth dripping with blood. His face sported a multitude of deep gashes from the huge knuckles of the beast that had pushed through his skin. He spit the blood from his mouth as he slowly worked his way up from the pavement, knees wobbling and both hands holding his gut. A gentle wind blew across Joe's face. A ghostly voice filled Joe's ears. "You have not failed yet, my boy. Remember what I told you. You possess the power that the beast cannot withstand. Look to your heart for the power and you shall be victorious."

Joe recognized the voice. P'an Ku had not left him to fight alone. Joe closed his eyes as he felt a new energy fill his body. The pain subsided as his thoughts turned to the loved ones that he must protect. "It's not over yet you son-of-a-bitch."

Massaging his gut, he pulled the tubes from his belt, placing one in each hand. Knowing it was do or die, he pulled himself to his feet. The pain in his side causing him to cough hysterically. With each cough he raised his body until he stood fully erect. To the surprise of the beast, Joe riddled him with blasts of holy water spraying his eyes, face and upper torso. The water reacting like sulfuric acid, the demon's skin began to bubble, smoke and burn. The demon reeled back in excruciating pain.

Again, Joe grabbed the next tube. Blowing with great power he blasted the demon's lower appendages. He repeated the process until all the tubes were emptied. He looked up to survey the damage. The water had done its destruction, but it wasn't enough to stop the demon's rage. The beast tore at his skin trying to stop the burning. The demon's agony raised Joe's spirits. He might have a chance now. Joe regained his strength and went after the demon. The beast caught a glimpse of the charging attacker. He pulled the melting skin from his face to clear his vision. His eyes met Joe's as he charged. "Oh shit, I'm in trouble," Joe thought.

With a fierce roar, the beast bolted toward him. Summoning all its blades, it began to slice and dice everything in its path. A large, green city dumpster disintegrated as the dark warrior made his way to his target. The monster's blades raked across the stone walls of the buildings as the alley narrowed, raining sparks over Joe and itself. Hot embers fell into a nearby trash can, igniting a fire that illuminated the alley.

Joe tried desperately to escape. No matter which way he tried to run, he was constantly cut by the tips of razor-sharp blades, leaving his back and arms slashed and draped in blood. A demonic arm slapped across Joe's face as it passed him to another waiting arm. It pinned him into the corner of a brick wall as a street lamp shimmered down over the both of them. Joe's hips were held in place with its two front legs. Two of its serpent-like arms aimed their bony sabers into Joe's lower ribs. As one arm grabbed the side of Joe's face, another reeled back to deliver the deathblow.

The demon gurgled with satisfaction. "I told you! You are no match for a god like me!"

Joe choked as his blood filled his lungs. "Go ahead, you will only send me to a place that I long to be. All that I love is there waiting for me. But let me ask you. What do you have waiting for you?"

The demon's laugh stopped abruptly. This question enraged the demon. It screamed in Joe's face. Knowing he had touched a nerve, Joe closed his eyes and with a smile of satisfaction, surrendered his life to the beast. A voice in Joe's mind told him, "Oil!" Joe recognized the voice and feelings that this voice was coming from his heart.

Just then, a bolt of immense energy blasted the right side of the demon's skull, releasing bellows of bright light. The force of the impact was so great that it sent its head into the wall next to it, shattering the brick and causing Celesthargor to release Joe. Joe slumped to the floor in exhaustion. He could barely keep his eyes open from the blood dripping into his eyes. He forced himself to look up and see what had saved him for the moment. To his amazement, there, hovering just above the ground was the most beautiful angelic figure of a woman he had ever seen. "Mihito. My grandchild." "I am here now."

His body surged with excitement as he realized his grandmother had come back. Joe now knows why his grandmother left him when she did. She needed to be here at this exact moment to distract the creature. The beast recomposed itself to face his new attacker. "You will not complete your mission" Joes Grandmother stated. "Now Joe… Now!" She told him.

The beast grabbed Joe's left arm and lifted him up off the pavement. Screaming at Joe's Grandmother it turns to Joe and again let out and ear-piercing scream into his face. Dangling in midair Joe trying his best not to heave from the stench coming from the creature's mouth, he ceased the moment; Joe was able to grab the PVC pipe mark oil that was in his right-hand pocket given to him by Father McNelly, placing it to his lips and blow with all his might. His timing could not have been better as the oil filled balloon slapped across its tongue and was shredded by the razor-sharp teeth. Joe still hanging in midair pushed off the brick wall near to him and kicked the beast in the throat and under it jaw causing it to involuntarily swallow the holy oil. The creature released Joe's body as Joe fall to the unforgiving ground below. To everyone's surprise the demon tried to throw up the holy oil which it ingested but to no avail, for it was oil and not the holy water that could possibly be washed out. The beast grabbed at its own throat and looked to the sky in supplication knowing it had failed and would now have to face it Lord in shame. He knew the fate that befell those who dishonored the Dark One.

The beasts' entire body started to tremor as hundreds of illuminating humanoid hands started to cut and tear their way out of the prison where they were held captive. The creature wreathed in pain for it could feel every nerve ending being ripped and torn from its body. Glass shattered and rained down from the nearby building and parked cars from its screams. It was now time for its pay back from all its victims it had killed. Clouds formed over the city as lightning crackled in and around them, as the beast was completely ripped apart, blood and unrecognizable internal organs litter the entire ally producing a vile stench that people five blocks away could smell it and wondered where it came from. The dark clouds open up as a beautiful beam of heavenly light descended onto the ally and music so beautiful it was beyond description filled the night sky. The spirits the escaped from the belly of the beast were invited home and their struggles were now over.

Joe's grandmother approached her grandson. "Know this. When your time comes, all of us that loves you and there are a lot of us, will be waiting to greet you." She kissed his cheek as he fell into an unconscious sleep.

Joe awoke the next day in a hospital bed, not real sure he believed what he had been through the night before. Was it all just a dream? If it was real, why was he no longer in pain? His ribs had been brutally crushed, his arm broken, his teeth busted; yet he felt no pain and no scars plagued his body. His doctor walked into the room. "Glad to see you're finally awake. Perhaps you could fill us in on how you ended up in an alley on the verge of death. And how you managed to recover from the worst set of compound rib fractures I've ever seen without a bone splinter to show."

Joe looked up at the doctor. "What are you talking about?"

"You were found last night in an alley not too far from here. You were in real bad shape. Several broken ribs had punctured your left lung. Blood poured from your mouth like you were spitting up water from the internal bleeding. None of us honestly thought you'd make it through the night. Now here you are, sitting up, with just a few bruises on your face. The second set of x-rays we took early this morning shows that not only did your ribs heal, but we can find no trace of the breaks at all."

The doctor pulled the films from the envelope he carried and held them up to the light. "Are you into some sort of mystical healing religion or something? We sure as hell can't explain what you did."

Joe looked up toward the ceiling and smiled. "Yeah, you could say that."

Several days after the gruesome battle, Joe Jeager walked out of the hospital pushing his soon-to-be wife Michelle in a wheelchair. Tied to her wheelchair was a multitude of balloons of many colors and on her lap lay a teddy bear wrapped in a blue bow. As they wheeled into a nearby park, leaving the hospital he helped Michelle out of the wheelchair and struck up a conversation.

"Honey, we have a lot of therapy to go through," Joe stated. "You know, to help in our healing."

"Okay," Michelle smiled and replied. "To start us off on the right track, I have something for you."

Joe looked with curiosity. Michelle handed Joe a small teddy bear. "We're going to have a baby boy!"

Joe's eyes lit up. "Oh yeah!" Joe yelled and he wrapped his arms around his love.

Michelle pressed her head deep into his chest. "Listen, a few days ago I had a strange dream. I felt the warmth of two hands rubbing gently across my face. When I opened my eyes, there before me was an angelic figure. As my eyes focused… You're not going to believe this, but it was your grandmother! She smiled and told me, 'You're going to be fine. It's not your time.' With a smile she stated, 'you're going to have a healthy baby boy! Life will be fulfilling. Love each other! It will be your strength.' And I will always be there; she leaned over and kissed me, then moved away from my bed and into a brilliant light and disappeared into the floor. That's when I came out of a coma." "Later that same day the doctor came into my room and told me the great news about the baby and how healthy he is!

Joe looked at her and a smile spread from cheek to cheek as he quickly grabbed and kissed her.

"Owe! Owe!" Michelle replied.

"I'm sorry sweet heart." Joe stated.

As they both giggled and held each other.

"I love you with all my soul." Joe replied.

As he walked Joe stated, "I'll think I'll buy him a brand-new fishing pole."

Michelle playfully slugged him in the shoulder. "Don't be silly! I hate fishing."

Joe looked off into the distance. Finally, he could now start to get on with his new life. As they walked through the park, Joe felt his breath being pulled from his lungs. His chest grew tight as he grabbed at his shirt. A voice fell on his ears only like a grunted whisper "This isn't over with, boy. You had better be prepared; my next warrior will not fall me so easily. My reign is near. Evil will prevail."

As the voice faded into the wind that carried it, Joe looked up at Michelle who seemed not to have noticed what happened. Joe realized that he had a new friend. It wasn't over, Satan would forever watch him. Joe would never have a normal life. He now knew he was meant to suffer divinely for the fate of all mankind. He known deep inside, there is another one he will have to deal with, soon.

THE END